GW00601406

Crannóg 59 autumn 2023

ISSN 1649-4865
ISBN 978-1-907017-66-7

Cover image: *Révérence, 2017 by Julie D'Amour-Léger*
Cover image sourced by Sandra Bunting
Cover design by Wordsonthestreet
Published by Wordsonthestreet for Crannóg magazine @CrannogM
www.wordsonthestreet.com @wordsstreet

CONTENTS

Submissions for Crannóg 60 open November 1st until November 30th
Publication date is March 29th 2024

Crannóg is published bi-annually in spring and autumn.

Submission Times:
Month of November for spring issue.
Month of May for autumn issue.

We will <u>not read</u> submissions sent outside these times.

POETRY:
Send no more than three poems. Each poem should be under 50 lines.
PROSE:
Send one story. Stories should be under 2,000 words.

We do not accept postal submissions.
When emailing your submission we require three things:
  1. *The text of your submission as a Word attachment.*
  2. *A brief bio in the third person.*
  3. *A postal address for contributor's copy in the event of publication.*

For full submission details, to learn more about Crannóg magazine,
to purchase copies of the current issue or take out a subscription,
log on to our website:

www.crannogmagazine.com

This issue is dedicated to the memory of

Patricia Burke Brogan

who passed away in 2022

Mandy: What happened, Cathy? You didn't – did you – you didn't try it again?

Nellie-Nora: Mother o'God, Cathy! Did you?

Cathy: Mmn! *(Moans)*

(The women resume work. Pause.)

Cathy: *(slowly)* After Mass – while Mother Victoria – was serving Father Durcan's breakfast – I hid in the Confession box! Father Durcan left to collect his car. He never closes the front door. – He drove off without closing the main gate either! I hid behind the beech tree! And I got out! Out on the main road!

Mandy: Outside? Oh, Cathy! Outside!

Cathy: Yes! Outside on the road! But I was like this! No coat! As I walked up the hill, I could smell the sea! The sun was shining on me at last! – A fella passed on a bike – whistling!

Mandy: A fella whistlin'! Oooh, Cathy, what happened? Did you see any smashers when you were out?

Cathy: No smashers, Mandy! No! A few children pointed at me, laughed and called me names. A laundry van passed, turned around and came at me. I fought. I bit them. I screamed. – But they brought me back. – Mother Victoria gave me a mug of strong tea and the usual sermon! *(She rubs her head.)* – But I'm getting out! I'll keep trying! I'm getting out!

from *Eclipsed* Act 1 Scene 3

Dear Scribe

Maureen Weldon

Like an assignation under a full moon,
I can't get enough of your beauty.

Yet you speak of great suffering,
of hunger, of death
of a people so dear to my heart.

Dear Scribe
your truth in dark corners shines, glitters bright.

When I Showed You the Poems I'd Written About You

Ilse Pedler

I said it was because I wanted your permission before I shared them
with others
but what I really wanted was your forgiveness.
You said you'd look at them when you were alone,
when you felt strong enough but it was OK, it was my story too.

Weeks later you said you'd read a couple but stopped
because they'd made you cry and you didn't want to cry.
I said I never wanted to make you cry.

I said I wrote the poems to try and make sense of things,
to place words, like sutures, across the wounds,
join verses together in long strips like bandage.

I wrote about a boy in a turret, gold spinning
from his hair and not being able to reach him,
you said, imagine what it was like to be that boy
alone in a turret, looking out of a window
at everyone so far away.

I wrote about the same boy, a spell upon him, closed
from us behind a screen of thorns, our lives desolate with waiting,
you said you imagine what it was like to be that boy
unable to move as the briars grew towards you,
feeling the prick of them, like daggers on your skin.

I said at least you were loved, all three of us loved you,
you said you knew, but it was missing the point;
maybe some days you wanted to carry on watching TV and not pack
an overnight bag,
maybe some days you wanted to go to a friend's house after school
and not ours or hers
and maybe some days you wanted to say what you really meant
without
worrying about taking sides
but it didn't matter, it was all in the past now,
I said I was sorry; we thought we were doing the right thing.

Here we are thirty years on still trying to make it alright.

Spring

Ivy Bannister

Sunlight and wind scour away winter's decay
as branches sway. A blush of newborn green.

On the wall there's a thrush, intent beside a sprawl
of jasmine. In a whirr she dives deep into the vine,

surfaces at once, an object dark and big and round,
scissored in her beak, then she drops to the ground

near the bricks that edge the flower bed,
where on sapling legs she darts and dances,

swat, swat, swatting her prize against the brick.
Shrapnel flies. No seed pod this, but a gastropod,

half-in, half-out of his shattered shell.
Her beak, a guillotine that falls and shreds

his plump grey smugness into tatters,
meat for her blood and bones. Replete,

she looks to the sky, lets fly a blaze of song.
Feathery Amazon, queen of the spring.

Summer, 1976

Hugo Kelly

IT WAS THE SUMMER TO END ALL SUMMERS. The earth dried hissing bursts and then bloomed as if some hidden reservoir of life had burst. The briars on the roadside knotted in ferocious green strands, airy flowers blossoming amongst the thorns. Hoverflies and crane flies buzzed the air in chronic movement and cabbage white butterflies moved like spinning petals through the warm air. Creamy cow parsley grew tall along the verges and the cattle lay in the pockmarked fields, tails flicking the air with indifference. On the coast road, car engines growled in the heat, their radios whining through the open windows. We were staying in a cottage rented for the summer ten miles from our town and it was a new existence for me. I woke early every morning and felt suffocated by the heat and the silence and by the lack of company of my own age. There was no shop for five miles. We had no television. I could not believe we had to live like this.

My parents were different too it seemed to me. For a while there had been tensions with my brother who had taken up a job as an electrician in Sligo. Our small family were changing though at the time I did not understand this. In the country my mother seemed happy again. She wore bright dresses and an exotic red head scarf as she hummed her way about the cottage. It was an old place, aged and unkempt. Thick cobwebs hung in corners and there was the unmistakeable rattle of mice. The fridge barely cooled its contents and milk always seemed about to turn. When I complained my mother did not seem to care.

'You won't starve,' she said.

'I hate it here,' I said.

My mother just smiled. I found her indifference startling. The news on the radio talked about a bomb in Belfast and my mother sighed. She turned off the radio and lifted her book.

'Your father will be here soon,' she said. 'He will have some groceries.'

My father did arrive from work with some eggs and tins and a packet of unexciting digestive biscuits. My mother greeted him with a kiss and before having our tea he suggested going for a swim.

I thought of the cold, silty water and the greasy seaweed that covered our local swimming spot. I said that I would not swim. But to my surprise they went anyway and desperate for diversion I followed at a distance seemingly forgotten. It was seven o'clock and the air was still balmy. My father walked with his hand across my mother's shoulder touching her tanned bare arm. We made our way down the overgrown path, squeezing past the prickly whin bushes to the shoreline. A heron rose from the inky water and there was the plop of fish jumping before stillness settled again. My parents changed behind a giant black boulder and then threaded their way hand in hand across the matted seaweed into the sea. Neither were strong swimmers but in the water they seemed happy. I played around an old fibre-glass boat, disturbing the tiny crabs that scarpered away. I looked back and saw my parents in a tight embrace within the still water. They kissed deeply and I felt my body burn.

It was only then they seemed to remember my presence.

'Tom, go home,' my father said.

And so I left.

I walked back along the road towards the house. Stray beetles battled across the road catching in the warm tarmac. A grey plume of smoke rose like rope in the back hills. I thought of running away, thumbing a lift to town to visit my friends. I imagined the small-town park where we shyly played rounders with the girls. I thought of the busy streets and the welcoming chime of shop doors opening and the inviting lines of magazines and comics to scan. There was no respite here and I felt desperate. My parents were happy and did not care that I was not. How could things get any worse?

Three days later with the sun still blazing my brother unexpectedly turned up from Sligo. He calmly announced that he had left his job. My parents were horrified. How could he give up a good job? What was he going to do?

He did not flinch in the face of all these questions.

'It's better that you don't know,' my brother replied.

I had never heard him speak with such firmness. He did not care about my father's rage and my mother's tears. He was a new person, so firm and resolute that my parents seemed cowed by him.

I was banished from the room and stood outside in the evening light beside the overgrown rose-bush with its winding stems and smudged pink flowers. A bee moved by with a nasal drone. A pair of bullfinches rustled and squawked in the fuchsia. I retreated along the crumbling path where I observed a nest of straw-coloured spiders crawling in all directions. Above me a bat flitted by and there was the sound of distant voices where far-off neighbours walked the fields. The pulse of nature beat in every blade of grass, I thought. I was frightened of its overpowering intensity and felt exhausted as if I had experienced so much that day. But when I thought about it, I had done nothing at all.

Later when we went to bed the house felt so warm that we opened the bedroom windows wide. My brother stood smoking a cigarette, blowing the smoke outside.

The moon was visible through the wispy clouds. The cigarette tip burned as he inhaled and his outline would appear in the dark and then merge with it again as it dimmed.

'Why are Mammy and Daddy so mad with you?' I asked.

'I suppose because I want to do my own thing. They don't understand. I am no longer their little boy. That's your job now.'

'Are you staying long?'

'No,' he said. 'I have places to be.'

'Where are you going?'

He seemed about to speak but then stopped himself and instead sighed.

'This heat. We're just not used to it.'

In the morning I walked the short distance to the well to fetch drinking water. The sky was already a hard gleaming blue. I dipped the bucket along the crumbling edges of the well and half-filled it as I had been instructed to do, enjoying the splash of cold water on my hands and sandalled feet. I carefully fished out the trapped midges and tiny clover leaves that floated on the water surface. Nearby a donkey brayed in protest at nothing. A purple dragonfly basked on the stone. Nothing moved. Already the day seemed stupefied by the sun.

Further along the road the sally trees grew in a profusion of spindly limbs and tongue-shaped leaves. Within this mass of growth I caught a glimpse of shining glass that blinked at me. I left the bucket where it was and walked along the grass verge, finding a large gap amongst the sally bushes that led to a gate. But there half hidden from view I came upon a car with the doors fully open like a set of wings. In the front seat a guard sat with a pair of binoculars lightly grasped in his hands. His eyes were shut as he dozed in the heat. I stood, unsure of the situation.

I felt I had done something wrong by discovering this guard though I could not quite understand the logic of this feeling either. As I stepped away I did notice that he had a clear view of our house over the fields.

The house was still tense when I arrived back but my parents had moved on from anger. Instead they were trying to engage with my brother. They talked of his friends and the social life of the town. My father said he could insure him in the car. They asked him to stay and have a holiday and said that there was still time to enjoy this weather. My brother's replies were non-committal and distant but I felt that normality had returned. Perhaps it was because of this finely balanced calm that I decided not to mention the sleeping guard.

Clouds came in and the day grew humid and unexpectedly there was a releasing fall of rain. Within a couple of hours a hazy sun had appeared again and we sat on our deckchairs. The radio played the top-thirty hits. The heat increased and everyone dozed, numbed it seemed by the sun. I felt restless with a strange sense of failing. I reasoned that I was not advanced enough to enjoy this summer. Instead I rambled about the overgrown back garden where an ancient shed had long since fallen in. There in the corner I found some blackcurrant bushes that were in fruit. The inky berries were heavy with juice and I picked them carefully into a pot. My brother nodded his approval at my work and later in the evening we went out to the top field and picked mushrooms, a foraging task he always enjoyed.

When we returned I could see that my mother had been crying and yet she greeted us with a smile. For a moment my brother seemed to hesitate before her. His face lost its assurance and he mumbled that he would cook the mushrooms. In the tiny kitchenette he wiped them with a damp cloth and cut the stalks before slowly frying in bubbling butter on the old black pan. Beside him my mother rolled out some pastry with an empty bottle and made a blackcurrant tart sweetened with apples and spoons of sugar that she cooked in the old gas oven. Later we feasted on the mushrooms, mopping up the salty flavour with thick slices of white bread.

This was followed by the freshly baked tart scorched with caramelised sugar and the dark sweetness of the blackcurrants.

My brother was suddenly content and seemed himself again. He joined with my mother and they hesitatingly sang 'Red is the Rose' while my father hummed along in encouragement. I belted out The Bonnie Banks of Loch Lomond, and everyone clapped.

The sky slipped into an ethereal blue, inky yet holding the light of the day like a low flame in the cover of its hand. We were happy and I no longer felt alone.

That was one of the last times we were ever together as a family. My brother left as he said he would a few days later and then some two months after that he was killed in an incident along the border near Derry. His sudden death brought an end to those summers. We never again took the house in the country or my parents did not swim together. We stayed in the town and met the sympathetic faces of neighbours who did not know what to say to us. Years later I would become angry with him for his selfishness. Some talked of his idealism but those words always left me cold.

In time I have made peace with what happened and the fracture that occurred within our family. Many make wrong decisions. And many like my brother do not get to enjoy the span of a whole life. Or savour the breadth of time that adds up to an existence. Instead there are moments that are significant within themselves. These days or evenings or hours gleam like a star around which the rich memories coalesce. That summer with its intense richness and its burden of heat is one of those. We sit amongst the falling light, our soft voices straining in song, the summer evening breathing around us in all its variance. There is peace in that.

At the Aquarium

Lucy Bleeker

I am a conger eel. My body three metres long snakes around this tank, tail
half-eaten by my friends as I have half-eaten theirs
in our ondulation to the surface.

I open my jaws to gloved hands throwing sardines and
anchovies. I catch my prey at nine, twelve and three and ferry the bodies to
my hovel in the wall, watched by human eyes beyond the glass.

You are a moon jellyfish, across the floor, *Aurelia Aurita*, floating
in the dark water. No heart, no brain, no eyes, no skeleton.
You threaten only a mild sting.

I watch you from my waters,
push the air from my gills and
covet a taste of your flesh.

Chained Male

Mary Turley-McGrath

The man in the chain mail suit turns
his back on the viewer;
he does not want us to see his face
or any face that he may have to kill
in the heat of battle or in cold blood.

Chain mail shrouds his head, long neck
and slight shoulders; he is a young man
and this, his first suit, weighs him down.
He feels stifled by its mesh over a light
linen tunic; sweat drips down his chest
and thighs; his face and hands are cold.

He thinks about days on the Ávila hills
with his new falcon, training her to fly
for the meat, seeing her go the length
of the creance to the perch; feels a jolt
to his body as she strikes his glove.

Rain Man

Louise G Cole

He sets out to claim her, tame her, take
a hold of Rain, enlists the help of Hope,
Faith, Science to capture the unruly run
of her, to do his bidding, earn her keep.

Wild, she is a keen, pretty thing at times,
and in a certain light, but look here,
she should work harder, keep at filling
oceans, winter turloughs, rivers, streams.

Whatever it takes to hold her, he will
harness her power, calm Rain's savage streak,
that puddle splash, rainbows over waterfalls,
surging torrents under the city bridge.

He'll have Rain wash the world in ways
she can only dream of, every needy bucket,
bowl and barrel filled full, she'll think
it's what she's born to, what she wants.

He plans to send her on exotic errands
beating sand from the mats of desert drought,
laying claim to blackened bush fires, slaking
the thirst of feckless forest leaves.

With full control of her he'll marshal clouds
from summer beaches, top up reservoirs,
drizzle growing crops with just enough,
stop her moving when he's had his fill.

But Rain can't be broken like flesh and bone,
or bought with empty promises, lip service.
She shies away from force, turns her wiles
to different guises, hair snowflake-braided,

slipping on frosted feet, she pours through
flood plains, won't relinquish free will,
drifts as slabs of arctic ice, blows steam
from geysers, strikes a deal with Wind.

Rain knows what Man wants, but she won't
comply, falls to her knees, open-mouthed
with cunning, births another violent storm.
It takes Man's breath away. Again.

Domestic

Carolina Corcoran

Finest china, morning-picked fruit seedy-sweet
tender to pulp with nothing but tongue against
roofmouth.
                    Their grandmother's garden
a maze of cane prickly needing no help
to remain upright unlike the weakling
peas and beans, even the warrior sunflowers
twine-wound.
                    Laterlife
he'll cut her down, drag hairwise, her spindly knees
across carpet, concrete, and she'll keen raspberries
for weeks.

Novel Excerpt

Mike O'Halloran

New York City 1983

ON FRIDAY AFTERNOONS THE LOBBY of the Cheshire hotel was busy with the arrival of well-heeled weekenders from upstate, and vaguely intimidated mid-westerners making their first ever visit east. Fiona liked the bustle and the banter with the new guests, many of whom had visited or planned to visit Ireland.

On that Friday afternoon, at exactly 2.30, just after she had checked in a couple from Minnesota, who were walking towards the lift, pulling a roll-on suitcase each behind them, the burst of sadness which rose within her was so powerful she felt like she could wail her head off. With this came the sensation that all her energy was being sucked out of her, through her feet, and that she was about to fall. Ten minutes later she was in a taxi. Images of Jimmy succeeded one another in her head, like waves breaking against a rocky seashore in a storm.

Back in the apartment she threw up twice before she finally drifted into sleep.

She woke. The bedroom pitch dark. A siren going off somewhere. A second later the knowledge burst over her. Stark. True. He had met someone.

She turned the alarm around to face her. It glowed a dirty orange. It was 3 on Saturday morning. So, she reckoned, it was 9 already back in Dublin.

It was 9 in Dublin on Saturday morning, and he'd met someone the previous day and they both already knew it was serious. She wondered which one of them initiated everything. Probably the woman. From the other side of the ocean, she could feel the strength of their attraction for each other. She was certain the woman was dark-haired. She wanted to know her name.

It came to her that the collapse of her energy the previous day must have occurred when he met her; as if a part of Jimmy that had remained lodged in her own being had retreated, pulled itself out of her so as to gather the energy needed for this new woman, this new love.

She placed a hand on her abdomen. It was freezing.

The city was still warm in September, but her teeth were chattering. She rummaged in the wardrobe for her winter dressing-gown, tiptoed into the kitchenette so as not to wake her housemate, Samantha. Boiled a kettle and lit a cigarette. The tears she barely knew she was crying flowed down her cheeks and onto the cigarette's filter. She felt a strange mixture of clarity and sadness and relief.

Six weeks later at a Thanksgiving party in her friend Jackie's apartment in Brooklyn she met him. The apartment was cramped with people, many of them Irish, and many of them illegal. She went out on the balcony to get away from the noise and her instinct was that he had followed her. Shane was from Blackrock in south Dublin. He had done a B. Comm at UCD, then trained as an accountant. An uncle who ran a chain of three bars in mid-town had sponsored him for a green card.

Her first thought about him was he might well have met Patrick on the rugby pitch playing in the schools Leinster Cup. Her second was that he was a nice guy.

'I wanted to see the States and get some experience before returning and starting up back home. What about you?' he said.

'I'm not sure what brought me here.' She felt sly giving him an evasive reply. But New York, she had discovered early on, was that sort of place. Lots of people went there because they wanted to, and lots came to escape something. She told him she worked in the Cheshire.

'A receptionist? So, you've got heaps of patience. Yanks are very demanding customers. Not like us Irish. We put up with anything.' He was smiling at her. And she saw in his eyes that he was appraising her. She was doing the same. He's not bad looking and he's got a good chat-up line. She wondered what it would be like to let her head fall into his chest.

'How long are you here anyway?' she said.

'I came out in '80. I'm thinking of going back next year. Things are bad at home right now, but I don't want to make my life here.'

'Neither do I.' The words tumbled out, surprising her. The answer to the question that had bopped along the edge of her consciousness without ever getting worked on, had been there all along. She felt playful. 'Be a gentleman and get a lady a glass of wine.' She handed Shane her empty glass.

He went inside. Fiona looked out across the balcony towards Manhattan, on the other side of the river, adorned by an army of lights sparkling in the night sky like a galaxy. She had seen the view from Jackie's many times. This time, however, there was something exciting in the view of Manhattan at night that until then she hadn't allowed herself, or perhaps could not allow herself, to feel. It was easier to let herself be carried away when she knew she could return home, than if she thought New York was a life sentence. The balcony suddenly filled with some of the partygoers from inside; their boisterousness irked her. She wanted to keep the balcony with its view all to herself, and Shane, when he returned.

She recognised some of them from previous parties. The two brothers from Cork who were UCC graduates. They'd come out on visitor's visas and now worked on building sites. There was the slight, auburn-haired woman from Dublin's southside who had told Fiona she was a graduate of the College of Marketing and that almost her entire graduation year had flown to the States, where many of them now worked illegally.

Fiona buried her face in her handbag, pretending to search for her cigarettes. She didn't want auburn (which was how she called her in her mind) to come near her. Auburn had broken down in front of her once already. She had cornered Fiona in Jackie's during the summer and told her she'd got a call from Dublin to say her grandmother had been diagnosed with cancer which had spread to several of her organs. 'I never thought of this when I flew here,' she told Fiona. 'I never thought I'd not be able to go home and say goodbye to my nan, that I'd never see her again. You don't think of that when you come here. You only think can I get a job, and will they make me legal eventually, or will I end up being taken to JFK in handcuffs.' She'd told all this through hiccupping sobs and tears, and it took what seemed like ages for Fiona to gently extricate herself and go chat to someone else. Auburn hadn't evoked much sympathy in her. Rather, she had served to remind Fiona of the time of her own grandfather's death, a time that rivalled her coming to the States in its bleak unforgiveness.

'Will you miss all this when you're gone back?' she said when Shane returned. She gestured towards Manhattan.

'Yes. But not that much.'

'I will, but it won't stop me from going home.'

He's going to ask me out and I'll agree, she said to herself. A memory came to her. Adrian. A brainy, lanky boy from Clontarf whose ability to have opinions on everything really impressed her. The first boy she had ever kissed. She was 14 and was at the Irish college in Falcarragh for a month in summer with Caro. She and Adrian promised they'd love each other ever after, but when he cycled out to meet her in Howth three days after returning home from the college, they struggled to find anything to say to each other.

'It's getting cold. Would you like to go inside?' Shane said.

Later, he asked her out, as she knew he would. Towards the end of the night, he came downstairs with her and Samantha, and saw them into a cab.

At first, they dated once a week. They could only meet for dinner on weekdays, as she was rostered to work the weekends and Shane worked weekdays. She liked the enforced slowness of their dating. He didn't push her to see her more often, and he had a relaxed manner that made him easy to be around. Mature was the word that came to her mind when she thought of how to describe him. He was a couple of years older than her, but the feeling he gave off was of being a lot more than that. She couldn't imagine him ever doing something rash or making a show of himself. In comparison to most of the Irish she knew in New York, he drank moderately, one or two bottles of beer over dinner, while she might have several glasses of wine. He was, when she thought about it, a man in control of himself.

She wondered ...

Since meeting Shane, she often found herself remembering how she and Jimmy had planned on going abroad. The memories no longer stung. They were pleasant, fanciful reveries in which she and Jimmy made their plans on long walks across Howth Head, or over spaghetti meals in the flat in Clontarf. When she imagined all this, there was none of the fear and worry she had felt back then. And in their place was substituted a feeling of wistfulness at the knowledge she was saying goodbye to a much younger part of herself.

The night before her fourth date with Shane, she decided she would tell him how she'd come to the States. Shane was a supporter of Fianna Fáil, and its charismatic leader Charlie Haughey, who he believed was Ireland's best bet to sort itself out. Shane was no radical, but he understood where the hunger strikers had been coming from, and his gut political instincts were for Britain to leave the north of Ireland.

He'd have got on well with my grandfather, Fiona thought.

She told him.

'I'd have followed you to the States,' he said when she had finished.

During a quiet spell at the Cheshire's reception desk the following morning, she daydreamed she was walking across Howth Head. This time, with Shane. She imagined it was a Saturday afternoon in mid-winter and there was a light mist around and the sea down below was grey, and you couldn't see the tips of the mountains in Wales, though when they looked back, they could make out the greyish outline of the mountains down the coast in Wicklow. They both wore warm winter jackets and jeans and when they came down to the harbour they turned back up Abbey Street and went into the Abbey Tavern where the fire was blazing and they got a table near it and they drank creamy delicious Guinness and ate fresh cod and chips and later they went back to the house they'd been able to buy with a mortgage that they'd no problem getting on account of Shane's practice and her being the daughter of a big politician who owned the Bayview Hotel and she hauled him onto the bed and told she'd come off the pill and she wanted him to fuck her to death.

Non-alcoholic

Polina Cosgrave

In the evening
I've no other drink
than the air between the pines.
My routine is that
of a stone's mossy side,
of algae hugging the pebble.
Oh light, let me go,
I'm all whispers and no words.
Shall we
sell this sunset
to someone better,
more pristine and diamond-like?

In my fishnets I slide
down the waterfalls of rage,
across the meadows of disgust,
and into a taxi's maw.
Drive, drive along the muddy stream,
with an expression hard as a rock in a throat,
but don't be fooled by my awkward step.
My knuckles are one solid scream of brass,
the rapiers of my heels are what
pierced all those holes in your moon.

I've only had the air between the pines
today,
and I seep through the ground
because I really want to.
Oh light, follow me,
will you.

When We Ask for Understanding

Maureen Curran

We ask with a bottle lobbed, a snowball pelted
with the spin of a hammer throw and
we ask with the chair tilted back, rocking on two legs
tightroping the gap between wall and desk.
We ask with graffiti gouged out
and inked in colourful tattoo,
we ask in the skipped pages of our notebooks
where a poet didn't say anything to us,
we ask with the unattempted answers
we ask with incident notes not signed in the diary.
We ask in vape and in cigarette smoke
curling question marks above our heads,
we ask in the flooded toilets, the pissed into bin
we ask with the lost schoolbags that keep us wandering
the halls after class has started.
We ask with the entries in the late book,
we ask with the video of the fight we post on Snapchat
we ask with the thick hate we lay on the other, other.

Liminality

Annie Deppe

And when the German doctor told me
he would see me again in two weeks,

I handed things over to him with relief.
If I sometimes think of my body

as a dear friend in which I navigate
the world, I also fear

not an inch of it seems quite trustworthy.
In the field below our house

a new pony has joined the older pair.
Flighty brown youngster.

A girl in a red shirt
strides across trying to calm it,

help it feel at home.
So much green. The rain

still approaching over the bay
but not yet arrived. My chance

to put down for even a moment
this heaviness. So much

green. The wind off the water
riffling the pony's mane.

Hennisweg

Liam Carton

'HENNISWEG,' SAYS HE. This auld fella's only one of many in this pub, but the many don't matter all that much to me when this one's the one who's all close by my side and nearly touching my ear with the stubble on him.

When he talks I feel the breathin' off him wet and warm against my ear and the smell of fags and stale Guinness washes around my head.

'Hennisweg and Heark,' says he and coughs across his knuckles like just the saying of it has taken something out of him. There are little spatterings of cream-coloured paint all across the backs of his hands and underneath his fingernails.

'Oh yeah?' says I.

'Oh yeah,' he answers, slow and rasping, and in case I don't get it he repeats himself all deep and pensive like; 'Hennisweg and Heark.'

Am I having a stroke?

I think that's just how people talk around here.

Himself looks like he'll topple if he lets go of the bar but he keeps upright somehow and just watches me, saying nothing. I'm careful not to look away from his bloodshot eyes. I heard that about drunks, that if you keep looking them right in the eyes, it suppresses the urge in them to slip behind you and bite out the back of your throat. I think it was drunks they said that about. Maybe it was chimps.

Eventually some sort of decision flashes across his face and he grins at me with an understanding that panics me.

'Sly, cunning, bastard young fella,' says he and I think he means it as a compliment as he backs up without even blinking and climbs all spiderlike and askanced up the wall. He looks away then, finally, fixes his eyes to the balcony above the bar and just hangs there, only moving with the shuddery inhale-exhale of his ribs. His fingers are sunk to the knuckle into the rotten wetness of the wall's plaster.

He ignores me, then. He keeps his eyes stuck fast to the balcony and after maybe an hour I feel safe enough to look away.

My pint's gone flat. There's algae grown in clusters where the foam was. Something surfaces, swallows a speck of ash in a quick flash of teeth and scales, then disappears again into the black depths. I look up to order a fresh one, but I've moved from the bar when I wasn't paying attention and now I'm a twenty-minute walk across the room at one of the low tables.

I try to catch the eye of the bartender but there's an old man already where I'm looking and when my hand moves, it's him that gets beckoned over.

He's close now. Skin and bones. Someone opens a window at the other end of the bar and the touch of night air almost knocks him to the floor. He has a pint already bought for me when he sits and grins a smile of yellow and plaque when he sets it down.

'Legs on ya,' says he, and before I can breathe an answer he has his fine leather shoe unlaced and his foot up bare on the stool beside me. Blue veins. Brown spots. The grin has stretched past his ears. It's then he shows me, while my hand flounders across the table for my pint, how the width of his foot from sole to ankle is thinner than the length of his finger.

'Esthe walking what did it,' says he. 'Walking the walls 'til yer feet scratch the cobbles flat, then walking them more 'til ye'r home for tomorrow's walk.'

'That so?' says I. I try not to sound it as a question but I hear the ask in my voice anyways as I say it.

'That's so.' He nods slowly, sharing something like an understanding. I duck my head, sup a mouth of foam and it barely misses me; hits the wall behind me and writhes. I can sense it reaching for the back of my neck but if I don't look back, that might just keep me out of reach.

There's dirt under his fingernails and a dead sheep out by the far corner of the beach. Probably it fell from the grassy slopes above but maybe it was pushed.

What a stupid thing to think.

Sheep fall from cliffs all the time. They chew the grass that holds the sand together and they step to where the ground flows like water around their hooves and only when the wind is rushing past them do they realise what falling means. They hit the cliff once, sent spinning by that one bit of limestone sticking right out, and when the beach meets them they spread into a platter for the seagulls and the rats.

Sheep are daft like that.

'Too old now.' The old man breathes the smell of rot and the beach slips away from me. 'Too old to walk the walls. Can't keep the bastards back much longer.'

'The bastards?' Again, the question slips out of me without thinking.

'Immigrants!' says he. He seems about to spit on the floor but I reckon he realises that if he did, the force of the act might snap his neck. 'I'm too old now, can't hold 'em back. But ye'r young yet. And the legs on ya. Years of walking in ya yet.'

I try to sup my pint but the distance from my fingertips to my tongue is longer than my arm.

Oh God. Maybe the sheep really was pushed.

'Nish, lads!' calls a voice above us. 'Hup!' And an old man hops the balcony and snaps to a stop just above my head. He sways from the rafters by the noose about his neck and the fellas look up for a second, then go back to drinking.

That's just the kinda place this is. Old men kill themselves every day in bars like this.

'Walls fer walking,' says the man across from me. He takes another sup while back home his good fields fill with rushes and his farm tools rust. 'There's walls fer walking yet!'

In a place like this, you wouldn't even know you were dead until you toppled from the barstool.

I nod wisely and think before I answer.

'Heh,' says I, 'Hennisweg and Heark.'

The old man nods with wisdom in his eyes and we listen to the creaking of the rope.

Blackberries

Theodore Deppe

Summer seemed over until the two-weeks' gloom cleared
and glistening blackberries lined the roadside as if celebrating
the return of the sun god. A small breeze
as I walk back from my swim, and the berries are like those
of childhood, sweet bursts with tart sparks,

and what to do with all the real sorrows, the honest worries,
when the taste of berries at the corners of my mouth
starts me talking to myself, but I'm also talking to the world
that miraculously includes me, I'm turning
a circle in the road to take in seascape, mountains, and windblown fields,

and suddenly the twenty-one-year-old rookie who ruled
the Game of the Week five decades ago comes to mind.
Mark 'the Bird' Fidrych paced around the mound between pitches,
smoothing the dirt with his bare hand, then concentrated
by talking to the ball, telling it just what to do.

I pick a handful of berries to bring home to my wife,
wanting to tell her how fifty thousand fans chanted the name
of the most unlikely of stars, a kid who'd been held back
in first grade, then again in second,
and suddenly was grinning from the cover of *Rolling Stone*.

He partook of the supersublimity of summer itself —
that must be the word for it, if there is one, *supersublimity*.
He's gone now, but if injuries shortened his career
to one glorious year, his ebullience brought him to mind
half a century later. Joy has its afterlife.

Occasional Furniture

Mairéad Donnellan

Female civil servants holding established posts will be required on marriage to resign from the civil service
Civil Service Regulation Act, Ireland 1924

Before the wedding she was gifted
a faux rosewood cabinet
and a lifetime to fill it with whimsies.
At twenty she began her collection with curios
brought back by her father from the Bronx;
a set of sherry glasses, a green crystal sphere,
a commemorative vase from the Eucharistic Congress.

Relatives brought carving forks and fish knives,
velvet cassettes filled with silver things
that served no purpose in our home.
No one drank from her mother-of-pearl coffee cups
or the gold-rimmed goblets except ourselves
to heal childhood fevers with an elixir of whiskey.

Everything stayed as she had arranged,
we were content to watch pottery swans going nowhere,
her little nests of delph flickering in firelight
until we found the key to umbilical clips,
baby wristbands, a bead taken from an infant's ear.
We unfolded airmail stationery tucked behind a butter dish,
read details of fine weather sent in free-flowing hand
from sisters in upstate New York.

The white china teapot was wound countless times
so we could hear the the 'Bridal Chorus',
a hollow tune that played as it was lifted and tilted,
a sad note left suspended
when put back in its place.

Altonelvick Waterfall

Michael Farry

i
How strange that on this winter beach watching
my youngest grandson delight in wet and wind
I remember seventy years ago, being taken
by a grandfather who pitied a boy too quiet for advice
to a waterfall in our rough mountains and see
damp cliff and cleft, hear the smack of cold water
in front, the Atlantic behind. Something told him –
my interest in the quarry's rocky outcrops,
the fuchsia and wild orchids perhaps –
that despite my bookish ways and sober habits
I'd appreciate a glimpse of a wilder, untamed
mountain landscape recognizing something of himself.

ii
I call to mind that uneasy man, who taught me much
in his wordless way as I watched his arthritic fingers
manipulate willow and wood, stone and straw
sympathetic to his materials and task, appreciated
his trust in my young hands, his smiled corrections
and gentle example, offer gratitude a lifetime later.
I've gone back often, seen the cottage decay,
the hill road re-aligned, his orchard fruitless,

admired how their stubborn stone walls, church
and holy well survived, but the waterfall
was never part of the nostalgia tour,
forgotten like a shameful bone-break, old itch.

iii
He was happiest outside, on his knees, repairing
a boundary wall, a sheep gap, rebuilding
a faulty entrance, or sitting weaving
at the stable door, while I stood beside him,
handed him his chosen stone, selected rod
in awe of the stability he summoned from dry stone,
the solidity he conjured from those pliable willows.
Some days he'd let me add a rod, tell me where
to start, end, how to conceal the join, the trick
of bending without breaking. Long after Algebra
and Greek were forgotten, I remembered,
took time to weave a final monumental creel.

iv
If I had the courage, I'd dedicate that spot a haven,
build a cabin there against the cliff, to escape
a lifetime of providing, sing matins and compline
in harmony with the timeless water, live out
these last days happy in the shade, safely obscure,
mapping the complex routes by which
highland water travels to the sea in that land
where no broad rivers sweep through meadows,
no lazy trout hide in wide overhung bends, just
innumerable mountain streams steal furtive passages
by crumbling stone walls and neglected willow
towards the dark and fierce bulk of the ocean.

Eating Achilles

Jessica Grene

WHEN MY HUSBAND DIED, I thought I'd put him in the garden.

I told my sister this. She looked confused for a moment.

'Oh. Well, see how you feel when you get the ashes. You don't have to decide now.'

At that point I was calm. Some part of my mind was holding out. I didn't really believe that my husband had ceased to exist. My consciousness floated above the action, waiting for the finale. It watched me make arrangements for the service and cremation. That part of my mind was keeping the story for him. I was going to tell him, sweetheart, I had to decide where your ashes should go, God, it was awful.

I was going to scatter his ashes under the oak in the corner of the garden.

He told me he would put a swing on it for Achilles. He showed me the branch where it would hang. Light filters through the bright emerald leaves in dappled patterns in summer. I imagined Achilles, sometimes a blonde girl, sometimes a boy with dark hair, laughing and swinging high. There was a flower bed behind it, a profusion of blue and purple blooms. My husband said they were perennials, would come back every year. He laughed at me for asking would the colours change.

The planning part of my mind thought it would be a good place for his ashes. The floating part was thinking that he would have to tell me if human ashes were bad for the plants. The ashes would go into the earth, they would be absorbed into the roots of the tree. Some part of him would stay in the garden.

The garden was all his. He cut the grass, he planted the flowerbeds. He had planted some herbs and vegetables.

I can't keep plants alive. It was a running joke in the office. We each had a plant on our desks. Mine died. The replacement died. Anyone taking leave gave instructions that I was not to be allowed near their plant.

When I left my job, they presented me with an air cactus. A small rootless thing in a glass bauble. It survives blowing around in the desert. It's supposed to be unkillable. I don't know how I killed it. It shrivelled and went grey. My husband threw out its corpse.

'Seriously, how'd you manage that?'

'How am I ever going to look after a child?' I wailed, entirely joking. We were going to be amazing parents. I told him that we had to name our baby something character-building, like Achilles.

The room next to ours was Achilles's room. He teased me about how I would cope with baby-slime all over my carefully chosen furniture. I laughed, because I had made a family home. My style was vibrant, good-quality furniture. Our house was perfect for our family.

I hate us for agreeing that we had plenty of time.

My sister takes me to stay with her family.

My brother-in-law sits at the table chatting while my sister clears away the meal she's cooked. I used to catch my husband's eye when this happened, silent couple communication. Don't you ever pull that one on me, I told him.

He was never supposed to leave me to clear up the mess.

One evening, I look over at the sofa. The little one is on his father's lap, his brother nestles against my sister with her arm circling him. I suddenly hate their little family cuddling in the flicker of blue light. I say I'm going to bed. My sister moves to get up, to follow me and see if I need anything. I bark at her to stay where she is.

I couldn't keep the house, the garden and the oak tree.

'But we have life insurance.' I am stabbed with the memory that my husband always insisted it was life *assurance*. So pedantic.

The solicitor politely explains that yes, we had life assurance policies, but. Sad loss. Your husband's income. Costs. Significant disparity.

'I see. Thank you for explaining it.'

Fuck you, you stupid prick, I say to my husband. I get more and more enraged. How fucking dare he leave me like this.

The urn with his ashes stays on the mantlepiece. I moved the Aspara dancer relief to make room for it. I hate cluttered shelves.

Our beautiful house. The work that I put into it. The plans we had. We talked about Achilles, we had lots of plans for him. Or her. What if it was a girl? Even more character-building, I said.

Someday, I'd tell our daughter, our son, we used to talk about a baby, we called you Achilles before we had you. Now I'm the only person who knows that that room with the warm mango walls is Achilles's room. The bookshelf, the armchair, wardrobe, curtains and carpet.

I never really minded the teasing about my gardening skills. I did sincerely mean to keep those plants alive. I don't know what I did wrong.

'What if Achilles gets my gardening skills, and grows up colour-blind and messy, like you?'

'Babe, I have a normal person's perception of colour. And I'm bloody tidy by civilian standards.'

We laughed and were smug because we were golden.

I am so angry with him for all the ways that he was not perfect when he was alive. I am so angry with me for wasting time noticing them.

I don't want a thing from the house now.

Are you sure, my sister kept asking. Nothing, I told her. Not even? No.

Every chair, every shelf, every damn light fitting. I made a choice about each detail. It reflected us. I poured all my love, my creativity and energy into that house. It was our happily ever after. But it hadn't begun yet. No Achilles. No swing.

The last vestiges of my husband will not stay here when I leave. He is not going to return to the earth under the oak where the swing was supposed to go.

He's coming with me. I'll dig up a random plant, and his earthly remains can go into a cruddy plastic pot with it. I will bring it with me and watch it wither. When it's desiccated, its leaves crumble, or it's a sodden mess growing mould, I will throw it in the bin. Or maybe I'll flush it down the toilet. He can flow to the sea via a sewage treatment plant.

I don't know what kind of plant it is. It could be one of the weeds that are already choking up the garden, taking over gleefully because he is gone. I find a pot in the shed. I get a trowel and half dig, half chop and drag the plant out. I scoop up earth into the pot. I take the lid off the urn, shake the ashes onto a layer of lumpy garden soil. Some of the ashes puff out in a slight breeze, a dusting of my husband on the lawn. I put my hands in the pot and mix the ashes together, crumbling the earth into them. The texture of the soil is more repulsive than the ashes. I find a bag of compost, and tip some in.

It's a richer colour, a soft crumbly texture.

You have to get your hands dirty, he used to tell me.

There are black crescents of his incinerated body under my nails. He never cut his nails in a smooth line, there were always little angles in them.

I find a grim little flat. The once white walls are ecru with age. Clustered spots of dark mustard damp crawl from the corners of the ceiling. Its miserable square of balcony hangs over the road, a rusted can full of cigarette butts left on it. I carry the husband-plant in my arms to my new place. Like a fired employee clutching a filing box.

I buy the cheapest of everything in one transaction online. A bed, mattress, sheets, plates, table, lamp. The furniture is flat-pack, with veneer in varied unconvincing approximations of wood.

I water the plant daily. I'm giving it a fighting chance.

Our life together seems unreal now. Our wedding, our house, sex and meals and holidays. They all seem as fantastical as our never-conceived child on his or her swing. A montage of glowing moments that seem imaginary. These scenes flash through my mind, overly bright Technicolour in the sepia flat.

'You let me down,' I tell the plant.

All that seems real is my fury. My irritation.

The people in the bereavement group nod when I mention my anger. It's normal, they tell me, we've all been there. I'm angry with him, I say, and they are not shocked. Part of grieving, they tell me. I hate him sometimes, and they nod. I start to explain about his nails, and the shelves, and how he would call anything from periwinkle to navy 'blue', and their faces go blank, and I know it's not what they meant at all. I don't tell them about the plant.

The husband-plant doesn't die. Every night before I turn off the light, I tell it, 'Fuck you.'

You have to talk to plants, he used to say, they're sensitive to the human voice.

I talk to my husband, the plant. I tell him all the things he did wrong.

He wouldn't eat mushrooms, or anything that had mushrooms in it. Ridiculously childish. His accent changed depending on who he talked to, becoming fake north Dublin with men who called him 'Bud'.

My sister visits. She looks at the shoebox flat with its cardboard furniture, and looks at me, worried. I made her get rid of a pine table once, and scoured the city for the teak one that was right for her house. I keep my face blank, daring her to say anything.

She sees the husband-plant.

'Oh, that's nice.'

I tell her that I dug it up from our garden, and she nods, sympathetic but relieved. I don't tell her about the ashes.

One day a new tiny green shoot appears in the pot. Did it re-seed itself?

But the leaves are different. Some stray weed got in there. I leave it.

I stop saying 'Fuck you' to the husband-plant. This other plant is new and impressionable. Despite my corrosive thumbs, it keeps growing. I call it Achilles. It grows. It's not a dandelion. I wonder if it could be a tiny oak tree. I go into a garden shop and buy plant food. Achilles develops a cluster of green bubbles, berries or something.

My sister visits again.

'Oh,' she says, 'A tomato plant.'

It sneaked in, I tell her. It seems to be doing well.

I decide that Achilles needs his own space. I go back to the garden shop. A bag of compost, a bigger pot. I ask about growing tomatoes, and get a tomato frame. I show a picture of Achilles to the woman in the shop. I explain about my intruder, skipping the dead husband's remains part. I buy a trowel. I ease Achilles gently from the pot, careful of my husband's final resting place.

The green bubbles lighten, go orange and then red.

I wonder if it would be wrong to put Achilles tomatoes in a salad?

I buy a salad bowl. It's stoneware, a bright cobalt. I can't eat a salad made of Achilles served in a shitty cheap bowl. I keep it on the table, a vivid note in the middle of the drab box.

I carefully pick the ripe tomatoes and slice them. I pour olive oil on them, add salt and pepper. The juice from the tomatoes lightens the greenish oil to golden.

I focus only on the blue bowl, the red tomatoes dripping golden on my fork, as I eat.

I plant some runner beans on the balcony. Their scarlet flowers bloom in the summer.

Transmitter Road

Maggie Doyle

They landscraped the mountain to lay the road,
poured a concrete path between the moss and heather.
The broken stones underneath held on to their secrets,
Taking the weight of the years, not saying a word
About the latticed, steel towers growing on the summit.

Military hardware, keepers of the war stories,
Silver candles flashing in the night, sending and receiving
As the low flying iron birds hovered, chopping the air,
Squinting through the fog to find the rust rimmed nest
Where the devil wind goes screaming through the pylons.

The twelve kings beneath the cairn stones look down
On the metalled road where bog cotton still trembles
in the solstice dawn. They wait for the light to fill
the portal, lifting their Ard Brin horns to signal their
war is over and over and over and out.

A Matter of Degree

Angela Graham

Bucha, near Kyiv, April 2022

A naked woman in a fur coat, dead.
Condom wrappers on the floor above.
Whatever happened, it wasn't love.
Just scant words from the news but in my head
they kept on pressing to be understood;
something for me to grasp here, if I could.
The condom-users gone, a woman dead.
But why in fur? A pornographic hook?
She wanted it so much she chose this look:
deluxe seduction, high-class come-to-bed.
Is that the fantasy they made her play:
the lustful woman who leads men astray?

woman in fur coat condom wrappers dead
One click: The New York Times. She lay,
prone on a blanket, on backyard clay.
A short fur jacket pulled up to her head
hid her face. Her hair spread wide
like some sweet-dreaming debutante's. She died
in the cellar under the garden shed.
Long, muddy skid marks on her livid thighs

showed how she'd been dragged out. I realise
the cameraman had given her a shred
of dignity: she's naked from the waist
but a passing policeman blocks our gaze.

As my small mercy I will leave unsaid
the detail of her extreme exposure
to the men who, before they shot her, posed her
to make plain she was, to them, degraded.
Then they withdrew. Smart tower blocks look down
on the wire netting of the chicken run
where Mr Shepitko's trees spread
their bare branches over his smallholding
and the gloved young man focussed on unfolding
a green/pink chevroned cover for a bed
and the policeman stooping by her head
and the old buckets, ash heaps and that shed.

A naked woman in a fur coat, dead.
Those soldiers – they buried themselves in her.
Contempt, I see, is at the root of murder.
I search my conscience and I count my dead.

In My Pockets

Nicki Griffin

after Maura Dooley

Battered denim on the spare bedroom door: heart-shaped stone,
three hair grips, photo-booth photo of fresh-faced us, my body
fizzing in wanton desire.

Old waterproof squashed in the drawer that doesn't close: two Stugeron,
one Imodium, blueness of ocean on that Greek island holiday
where you asked me and I said yes.

Trench coat in the upstairs wardrobe: five tissues, four of them used,
fluffy mint out of its wrapper, those words I said I wish I hadn't,
and you wish I hadn't.

Long woollen coat, years old, that hangs in the porch: red woolly gloves,
two Rennies, a penny from before the euro, what I should
have given you, but didn't.

My father's favourite Harris tweed jacket: blister of used paracetamol,
dried seeds of honesty picked from the roadside, his good advice,
what I should have said to you, and did.

Drizabone behind the door: bus ticket for the journey home, sea shell
picked up on the way, much-loved purse I thought I'd lost,
your smile when you opened the door.

Selfie as Father's Melodeon

Breda Spaight

When asked to, Play us another one there, Erebus,
his right-hand fingers flick across his tongue,
moistly caress the white buttons
on my yellow pleated dress.

The Sacred Heart and kitchen chairs
eye each other, take to the floor
and reel together.
He squeezes my body.

When the dancers come
to a stop, he blots me of his sweat.
Melodies crinkle in the bag of sweets.
My body is a strapped black box

only my father can touch.
His arms sprout like pale shoots
as he positions me on the uppermost shelf;
my filigree face tuneless.

Tightrope to the Moon

Carella Keil

I MOVED AWAY. I GOT A TATTOO. It covers the scars. Not all of them. For those, I have you. You'll listen, won't you?

Bastet stares at me imperviously, jumps down from the windowsill. Slinks away. She's on her seventh life. Was she human in a past one, I wonder. Did she slip out of her skin, into another? Can I slip out of my skin, into another? Was she ever a bird? The way she looks at them with longing.

I would leap too, if I knew I could fly again.

My first life I was a mountain. I thought I would never die. I stared down at the clouds and up at the sky. One day a hiker tossed a rock off the edge, and I fell with it.

My second life I was the collective unconscious for a colony of ants on Mars. My thorax was the translucent blue of a marble, and my mandibles could bite through scars.

My third life I went back in time and was born again. I found religion that time too.

My fourth life I was a hawk. A lover brought me a feather, and I felt the wind course through my hair and a song like a lump in my throat. I kissed him until he cried.

My fifth life I got a tattoo of every name I'd ever known. I hadn't met you yet.

The sixth time I flew too close to the sun, and my particles scattered across the universe. You collected them. Most of them. Placed them in a jar. They danced, impatiently. Waiting for your touch.

My seventh life I killed a man. He was standing on one side of a trench, and I, on the other. His eyes were blue lakes until they filled with blood.

My eighth life I can't remember.

I fill the alabaster dish with milk for Bastet, listen to the sirens in the distance. Unlock the door, in case you decide to return tonight. She shakes her head. I lock it again.

Don't Be Like That Cindy

Aisling Keogh

IN MY HEAD, I COUNTED TO TEN and waited for her to leave the room. I could hear the pad-pad of her bare feet as she walked down the hall. The sniffling. The thunk-thunk of a three year old's protest march up stairs.

Follow her, follow her.

Any normal mother would follow their crying child upstairs. Hug them, reassure them. Give comfort, or whatever the fuck the necessary balm was to make sure they slept.

Instead of moving, though, I stayed stuck, thinking crazy woman thoughts.

Imagine if I slapped her.

Punching something would feel – I don't know. Because I know I could never slap Mia. But the wall, another person? That Tommy gobshite who'd called to the door to try and sell fibre optic broadband at bedtime, and precipitated her meltdown. Imagine her telling her daddy I'd slapped her. And my mam. And that bitch with the superiority complex at her Montessori. They'd call a social worker, they'd be right, too. And they'd take her away from me. Or he'd make me go, choose the toddler over me.

Hand curled tight, I rubbed my knuckles across and back over my cheekbone, erasing the kiss she'd left there.

I am a monster who prefers burning skin to my child's kiss.

Mia's kiss was one of those lingering, dribbly overstatements of a kiss. The sort that happens when a three year old says 'sorry', and truly means it. But I wasn't ready. I needed to rant, blame, take a bath. And some Prozac. And that is the shit no-one tells you about mothering.

All Mia needed was for me to say 'Everything is okay. I love you,' but I couldn't be the forgiving mammy today. Today, all that was on offer was the ranting monster, bargain basement mother, who isn't the best in terms of quality, but is serviceable at least. School lunches, nappies, dinners, the basics. No home-baked treats or shared reading time, and no paint-mess make and do at the kitchen table. It's no-one's fault, but I hate it.

I am more than this.

Yes, there are people worse off than me. First-world problems is what I have. A lovely home, a beautiful daughter, heat, food, and I'm moaning because I'm not fucking fulfilled. My granny and my mam brought up a dozen children between them. They weren't fulfilled either.

Outside, car door — front door, slam seconds apart, and Joe bounces into the room with a 'Hi, love. Where's Mia?'

Joe comes home at seven most evenings and plays the tickle monster game with his daughter. He makes her laugh, and then she cries because she's overtired, overloaded, overwhelmed by Daddy wanting to play. And then he tells me she's cranky and I grimace, and he laughs and says she must have caught the cranky off me, and he thinks he's funny – thinks it's funny – when I pull a face and turn my back to him.

And that's when he comes up behind me, wraps his arms around my waist and says my name. Says, 'Ah, Cindy. Don't be like that.'

Cindy is a doll's name, a doll whose bendy limbs are forever moved by other people.

If I was Tiny Tears, someone might hold me, soothe me. Tell me to hush – tell me everything is going to be okay. Someone who isn't Joe, because I want to tell him to fuck off – to not be telling me how to be. But I don't have the heart for a fight.

I can't breathe here.

And my heart is a soggy weight, full of tears yet to cry.

Joe stays standing that bit too long with his hands around my waist, clinging on to me in that needy way the kids do. I know what he thinks I need.

I don't want to.

My head is full of the fact that he can't link his fingers anymore when he wraps his arms around me, and since he can't, he holds on by pressing their tips into me, into the spare tyre I carry around with me. A spare tyre that's no use at all, when I get flat.

Usually, he lets go after a minute or two, and this buzzy silence bounces off the walls for a few minutes, then dissipates. Tonight, I pull away and shake my head at him.

'Don't.'

'Don't what?' he says.

Don't fucking touch fat monster me. Leave me alone. I just want everyone to leave me alone. Is what I don't say. I shrug, mutter something about baby-weight.

'Don't be like that, Cindy.' He said it again. Told me how to be. Again. 'You know you're beautiful,' he said.

I shook his arms off me, ran a sink of hot water and banged the pots around under the pretence of stacking them.

'Will you go up and settle her, tuck her in?' I looked back at him over my shoulder in time to see him not move. I kept my neck twisted, at that awkward angle, until it hurt. Still, he didn't budge, but stood there rocking on the balls of his feet, saying nothing.

'What?' I asked.

'She'd prefer you, love. You know that.'

'Oh for fuck's sake. Please, Joe?'

The kitchen door slammed. I plunged my hands into steaming water and pulled them out again as fast. Felt the sting and shrivel of too-hot skin. Joe could shove his kisses and compliments. If he knew what was really going on inside my head he wouldn't give them, anyway. He wouldn't like me any more than I like myself, let alone want me. All of which is grand with me.

He can go and fuck himself.

Today, sex was another thing on the list of things someone wanted from me, that I couldn't give. It was a sandwich and a snotty nose too much.

He came back into the room, then, Joe did. Came up behind me and put his arms around my waist, again.

'She's grand now, overtired is all,' he said.

'Well, whoop-di-do.' I said that bit out loud.

What did he want? A fucking medal for putting his own child to bed? And for just a few seconds I thought he got it, because he let go of me, and I thought I was free to move on – to finish the task at hand, proceed to the next one, and then the next, and so it goes. But then his hands landed on my shoulders and began to work their way down. I knew he was trying to help and the back rub was for me, but I can't accept the kindness because I am a fat, angry, lunatic mother, who still thought he was only doing it because he wanted sex.

I wanted to want him, I swear. I wanted to be like those women in glossy magazines and on television. Women who have jobs and lives and perfect houses and a sex life — and time to take those godawful relationship quizzes that I know are a pile of crap. I wanted to take them because I'm at a place where 'mostly c's' would feel like a win, and Joe's fingers can't take away any of this. But they must have done something, because while I'm thinking all of this I begin to breathe more deeply. Exhale, drift. Turn over possibilities.

I needed to wash the day off me, to sing in the shower. Drink a glass of wine. And I needed him to do the dinner and the dishwasher and feed the mutt. And maybe then I would feel like a normal person. And normal people have sex.

His fingers pressed into my fatty, orange-peel skin. I wished they would massage me out of existence. If tears could wash away the rolls of fat that changed me from bride, to new mother, to middle-aged housewife in six short years, I'd still be the perfect ten.

I'll need a shower.' I sounded as though there were hands gripping my neck.

'Okay, I'll do dinner.'

Gushing streams of scalding water turned me baby pink, rendered me softer. Because I needed softness, I only partly dressed afterwards – knickers, yoga pants, an oversized t-shirt, no bra. The yoga pants I'd only ever worn once before, at a fitness class I didn't go back to.

Don't dwell on it, Cindy. Don't think about that now.

Back in the kitchen, Joe told me to close the door behind me, and lifted an omelette from the pan. I moved towards an already open bottle of white in the fridge, and poured a large glass that was probably enough for two. While he faffed about with his phone, muttering something about a playlist, I took my first forkful.

Warm ham and feta, cut with spring onion, brought me back down, grounded me in the taste and smell of when life was better. From Joe's phone, the opening chords of an old 90s Manchester classic banished those years between Mia's epic meltdown and a time when we weren't always tired and broke – but happy living in a one-bedroom shithole somewhere near Mountjoy Square.

Joe, sitting opposite, was more focused on the plate than me. And I wondered if he'd abandoned any notion of love-making that night. And I wondered was I wondering out of nostalgia, or love, or duty.

When he saw me looking, searching for signs of something in his face, he stopped, full fork mid-air, and said, 'So, today kicked the shit out of you then?'

It was a question, matter of fact, no drama, but he was laughing too, and somehow that brightened the mood. There was light in his eyes, and creases around them that didn't used to be there, and it was love.

'I'll fight better tomorrow,' I said.

'No better girl,' he said, and I believed that he believed that.

And I thought about baby weight, the horrible sensation of fingers poking at the fresh-grown fat on my hips, him squeezing rolls of it while he thrust, and about how every time he moved inside me, I felt a twinge in my back, right where the epidural had numbed me for my first encounter with motherhood.

Still. Maybe.

'Better?' he asked, as I laid my cutlery on my plate.

A sigh and a smile. Relief, because yes, things were better.

I stretched backwards, arms raised over my head, and he ran his hand lightly over my stomach as he reached to collect my plate. I recoiled, then shifted in the kitchen chair to try and disguise my involuntary reaction to his touch, because I hated myself for it.

'You're beautiful,' he said. He'd noticed nothing. I smiled at him as he moved his hand away again, crossed the room and dropped my plate in the sink.

In the hall, a wail, a footsteps warning, before the kitchen door rattled with the weight of the small child on the other side. The handle slipped down and back up, made a noise, but didn't open. One small scream of childish frustration and everything I had spent the last hour pushing away came surging, crashing.

I can't move.

'Mia's crying,' Joe said.

'What?' I didn't hear at first.

'Outside the door, Cindy. Mia is crying. She needs you. It's okay, Mia, Mammy's coming.' Red-faced with frustration, he called out to soothe her. I was crying too.

'Cindy?'

And somehow Mammy found her feet, stood, opened the door. Hugged, stroked Mia's hair, led her back to bed, lay beside her in the dark, and cried and whispered 'everything will be okay', again and again – as though it was for the child.

And Mammy stayed there for ages after Mia drifted off, and never bothered going back to the kitchen or saying goodnight to Joe. She just went to bed.

Spellbound

Mari Maxwell

You smoothed the top sheet,
patted white cotton flat.
Hands like an iron slid creases out,
intent on your task.

And when you opened your eyes,
latched your gaze into the night sky
you assured me, no denying it,
God's light come to bring you home.

We wait all our lives for this.
Hearts engorged
lunging for a last breath
that forever stills our voice.

Siren's Throat

Daniel Hinds

Deep in the cave of your ear
– Ted Hughes, The Minotaur

Beneath the verdant top where she roosts
There is a maze of aeolian catacombs.

Lined with strings, the walls shake with her songs.
Her breath is felt even at the cave lip.

Despite her feathers,
I do not say this as the hen-pecked husband:

She knows everything, she tells less.

I say it as a suitor, first foot ashore.
Leather boot leaves a hard imprint on the coast.

I have seen flowers grow from sand
In the furrows of her claws.

I have seen invertebrate sea beasts scuttle
And crack the chitin of their shells in her wake.

The stone as pale and white as doves and Dover;
I am far from home.

I warm my hands on the chalky rock
And tear up my maps.

In her throat I hear the echoes of her lips,
The crunch of apple, and the laughter of her sisters.

When she spares me a thought,
Fruit tumbles and catches in the nooks.

I tie a golden thread to my chest hair,
Crack no more nails on the ascent.

When the next prow splits the shore,
I will be her minotaur.

Last Summer's Dresses

Jennifer Horgan

My yellow dress turns the water brown
I squeeze the darkness out
into the sink's shallow
Hang it, dripping,
over the bath
Last May, it swept the dry terrain
of an Italian villa
Covered the veins I hate,
ballooning Roman sun

Next, I drain, refill and dunk
the black and white one
Bought for the big event,
then downgraded – a mistake I think
In photographs, my breasts
in the borrowed blue, hang an inch
or two too low
Not the greatest show to put on
for an ex who almost broke me

Yes,
I wore this relegated dress
on our trip to Naples
Remember?
We ended up running down that platform like fools
I felt my month's blood drip as I tried to keep pace
with you. My breath, pushed beyond its limits
I croaked for you to stop, to turn round. You didn't
On board, I cleaned the blood off my legs
in a filthy toilet – then sat somewhere else.

It joins the yellow, both surprisingly unstained
Two soldiers, or at least, their uniforms, drying out

Joan Didion wrote about two dresses too, didn't she?
How they connected JFK's assassination
and the murder of that socialite
She said connections by dresses made as much sense
as anything
As with most things,
Joan Didion was right

What My Father Sees When He Looks Into The Mirror

Karan Kapoor

is a wolf, fangs and flesh. Blisters beneath his tongue,
violence drips like pus from one, another leaks
blood soft as fog. He unskins his wolfclothes
yet the shadow in the mirror remains.
Roses sprout from his underarms.
He feels he lives on the wrong side
of the mirror. Bats feed on his
infested wolfheart peeking through
his ribcage. His breath is the prophecy
of smoke. Seven pomegranate seeds fall
from each nostril. Elevator music
is humming out of his stomach.
The water he splashes on his face
fails to cool him. He no longer
delights in fire. Thirst, his primary
occupation. His tears fall in the basin
and the basin now has wolfeyes.
All his attempts of understanding
himself a feather heap of words.
The shape of his howl dangles
in the dark like a moon.

Even when he moves away,
the mirror babies his wolfshadow,
is blemished with the curse
of thirst. Who wants ants to carry
their body to the funeral? The law
of reflection: you see what is shown
to you. From afar, what do we
witness? A shovel in his wolfhand,
a crack in the mirror.

Beachcomber

Susan Elsley

THERE'S A GIRL ON THE BEACH in a long, white dress. She spins and her dress balloons like the bell of a jellyfish. Behind her the waves break. One foaming curl after another.

The girl comes closer, and I realise she's only a year or two older than me. She jogs backwards and laughs when the waves trickle over her feet.

I'm in my usual hiding place behind a rock where no one can spot me unless they come close. It's just above the tideline and Mum, in her teacher's voice, says that this salty edge is a precious habitat for plants. Today the sea pinks are an audience of waving pompoms while the girl dances, her feet pointing, and her head flung back so she can see the clouds.

You'd be surprised by what people get up to when they think they're not being watched. Last week a young man with a beard paced up and down before kneeling where it was damp. He shaped the sand into a mound and arranged pebbles on top. Then he stood up, brushed his trousers and strode towards the dunes. I went to look when he'd gone. The pebbles spelt the word, 'Help', so I wrote, 'Here', in the sand with a stick in case he came back. If Gran was with me, she would tap the side of her nose and say that he must be someone who lives one way but longs for another. She's wise that way, my gran.

Mum likes me coming here. 'Fresh air will do you good, Sorcha,' she says each time I head off to the beach which is a hop, skip and two fields away from home. She hands me a flask of hot chocolate and checks that I've got my phone and my purple woolly jumper. Her essentials for a girl who's been poorly.

I could tell Mum not to fuss, but I don't. When I get home, I show her my list of rock pool finds. The sea anemones, the tiny red crabs and the microscopic creatures that flit through the water. She says I should write a pamphlet about beach life to raise funds for the hospital that we have to visit every month, but I keep quiet about what I really do. How I watch people and scribble down what I guess about their lives.

The man patting the sand into a mound was the most interesting visitor until the girl. She looks like a princess out of a fairy tale with her billowing dress and her hair in braids. I touch the spikes of my hair which has started growing again. Mum said I shouldn't mind that it had to be cut off. It will be long and curly again in no time. Last week I confessed to her that sometimes I got scared in the middle of the night.

She hugged me and said, 'Don't worry, Sorcha, sweetheart. Other teenagers have had this, and they're right as spring rain.'

Her voice sounded like she was telling me what was for tea, but I saw a shiver go through her. The same one as when she comes out of appointments with my consultant. I smiled to make her feel better, and she held me tighter.

The girl screws up her face as if concentrating hard and stands on her tiptoes. Without thinking, I stand up, and balance on one leg too. I close my eyes. My breath slows. I hear the glug of the stream that cuts across the beach and the chatter of crows picking at the seaweed. There's a crunch of pebbles and then it stops. I decide to count to ten before I open my eyes. When I do, the girl is sitting on a rock a couple of metres away. She looks straight at me with eyes that are like Gran's. Ones that don't flick to the scar on my head.

The girl has wrapped the dress round her legs, and I was right. Her hair is amazing with beads like rainbow pearls woven through her braids.

'Hi,' she says, holding up a large shell. 'What's this?'

'It's a whelk. Hermit crabs live in the empty ones,' I say, and wish I hadn't. At school, they would have yelled that Sorcha, the girl with part of her brain missing, knows stupid things and I would have run and hidden in the toilets so no one could see me crying.

'Whelk.'

The way she says the word is different to me. Surer and with the sound of another place. She hasn't moved so I sit down because I'm feeling tired. This happens most days in the afternoon.

She strokes the shell. 'Cool. You're wondering, aren't you?'

'Yes,' I say, even though I'm not sure what she means.

'I don't usually tell,' she says.

She stands up and holds out the dress. There's a tear that has been mended with bright pink thread. I would have done that too. Made a jagged line because it's more interesting than the straight one on my head.

'Perhaps I'll tell you.' She glances at the notebook beside me. 'But you can't write it down.'

The moment she says that I itch to reach for my pen. This would be the first story that someone has told me, rather than one I've guessed.

'I found this dress in a cupboard in our new house,' she says, smoothing down her skirt. 'I take it on outings.'

'Like where?'

I see her smile stiffen as if she's not sure what to say. 'You know. Places.'

'That sounds fun.' I keep my voice light. I know people only tell their stories when they want to.

She stands up and moves away from the rock. She lifts one leg so it's higher than her shoulder. 'This place is awesome.' She drops her leg slowly. 'I might come here again.'

There's a slight rise in the sentence as if she's asking. Before I think, I nod.

'Brilliant,' she says, and bends over and touches her toes. 'Will you be here?'

'I'm around most days,' I say.

'Because you're a kind of beachcomber, aren't you?' she says. 'You watch out for people and gather stuff.'

I stare at her, wanting to ask how she's guessed what I do.

'I knew it. Secrets. We both have them,' she says as if she's discovered something that makes us the same.

Except she hasn't mentioned the scar. That's what everyone thinks is my secret even though it isn't hidden because the red line hasn't faded, and my hair is still short.

'I'm Bella,' she says.

'Sorcha.'

Maybe she'll lose interest now she knows my name. The girls at school keep away as if I've got a disease that you can catch by walking down the school corridor or hanging out after school.

I wait for Bella to tell me that she's got to go so I'm surprised when she says, 'Let's swop,' and turns away to pull off her dress. Underneath she wears red shorts and a rainbow-coloured T-shirt which I like even more than the dress.

She points to the purple jumper that Gran spent weeks knitting when I was first diagnosed. I wear it all the time as if it's my security blanket. I hesitate before she gives me that intense look again and I tug it over my head. When she puts it on, it looks as if it was made for her even though the sleeves are long on her arms.

I slip on her dress, and it drapes round my body like it's happy to be there. I kick off my shoes and run towards the hardpacked sand, and she follows, whooping. I gather the skirt over one arm, and skip in a circle, and she does the same in the other direction.

I make up steps, leaping and dipping as if I've always known what to do. I sing Ally Bally Bee, the nursery rhyme that Gran sang every bedtime when I was little, and Bella joins in. We scream out the words and scare the oystercatchers hunkering down by the water.

There's a couple walking their dog up by the dunes and they raise their hands and clap. The two of us wave back, not missing a beat. We dance until we've sung the song a dozen times. We jump more slowly, until we collapse on the sand and roll over and over.

My heart's beating like I've been running for hours but I don't feel tired anymore. I push myself up and bunch the dress under my knees.

Bella sits cross-legged.

'That was fun,' she says.

'It was brilliant,' I say.

She raises her arms above her head as if to stretch towards the sky then pulls her left one down as if there's something she's forgotten. Not before one sleeve of the jumper slips over her wrist, and I notice that she doesn't have a thumb or a little finger on that hand.

I keep smiling, looking straight at her like Gran does, and Bella hesitates before raising her left hand again. We both grin and I throw my head back like I never do. To show I don't care.

Haiku Éire '23

Noel King

---

derelict cottage
Bainin jumper unravelled
sheep snuggling in

ancient nun stumbles
on newly formed flagstone
by her convent gate

wind turbine
disappearing from view
– cloud falls

derelict convent
– black and white little bird
on the windowsill

Athlone lock, noon
barge in sand bank
waiting rescue

in the public library
the gold years lady
giggles at Roddy Doyle

Basset hound's eyes
knowing his master won't return
from Covid 19

Naming Her, Dusk

Anya Kirshbaum

I don't remember which one of us carried you
but we knew where we were going. Our tiny flock
scuttering over the sand, over the great drifts

of dying seaweed, the black flies flinging themselves
against our ankles, the suck and sink
of each step, that sharp and rotten stench.

I could see you — ghost you
glossy starred, salt water soaked, pants rolled, marvelling
at shore birds and hoping for a miracle
of whales. Whatever tender lonesome thing

that was in you, grandmother, also
in me, as we marched to the crevasse
where there was once a river running through, now
— a hollow mouth of driftwood and desire and all of us,
devotees.

I had built a dozen makeshift houses
on those downed trees — hours, rolling stumps for a table, chairs.
And there, we took a rope up the bluffs and in the blurring brush

dug a hole and somehow we left you. As though still children
ourselves — wild as the weather storming in, mumbling about the
shape
of trees as if we would remember, calculating the sturdiness of sea
cliffs,

imagining them more than a soul's scaffolding.
We made no map, instead digging as if replanting you.
Our fireplace urn, a small blue satellite

sent back. This the closest route we knew to devotion.
This because of you — bound and boundless
renegade daughter of birdsong, light-worn, storm-
blown, keeper of clear-cut forests and seaside Irish dreams.

Did we dig deep enough? We were never certain. We walked back
against the wind passing the shovel between us in silence.

Tiger Skin

Susan Lindsay

After Pam Fleming

Skin-tight is not the same as skint
or the skin-full
taken before sitting in the sleek car
powered by Esso. Feathered damsels
stretched on the bonnet lured
you to the purchase.

The petroleum company only needed
to commandeer that cat to say it all
under real bonnets
the most powerful feline imaginable
languid, poised, watchful, fuelled to spring,
snarl away.

The tame cat is not the same as the wild
spitting fur, yet may rub itself
on human skin
there's little to beat skin on skin
but faux fur, a faux-pas too far.

The shooting of tigers for skins
real desecration. Unreal.
Pas de chat, pas de chat,
dance away

that '... tyger burning bright'
everything to long for
the fabricated symmetry of its stripes
scrimped style and often skimpy

a skint world ultimate end
for human skin
slow fashion
re-design.

Finding True North

Elizabeth Power

I SUPPOSED SOMEDAY, but not when I was three weeks shy of ninety. Corpse cold and breathless, I lay there stunned.

'I'm not dead,' I shouted at that nurse. 'It's just – I can't catch my breath.'

Her reply was to close my eyes and shove a rolled-up towel under my chin.

Nothing for it so.

The children are taking my demise well. They are gathered on that old garden seat in the sun trap at the back of the house. Daughter one, Fusspot, has selected a photo from the photo album for the funeral director. It is a portrait of me with my blonde hair crimped, and those big blue eyes smiling into a good marriage and a certain future. I could dazzle then; my sisters were nothing in my light.

Daughter two, Loopy Loop, is writing my obituary. *At the end, the man who had a skill; a plumber to keep her warm, the cleaner who brought her two teabags in her tea, were more urgently courted by her than any high and mighty doctor.r*

'How's that?' Loopy Loop asks Fusspot.

'What do you think she'd make of it?' she replies.

Really, I couldn't have put it better myself.

Ah now, there's the Son, the one and only, brandishing my three-litre bottle of holy water.

'She'll have left the money to the church,' he says.

'She'll not,' Loopy Loop replies.

'Wanna bet?' He waves the bottle again.

By Gor. I paid enough to get out of jail free. A good few thou to clear the decks. It's not as though I'm a murderer or anything. My sins surely wiped long since with the devotion to Our Lady. On my knees in that cold church. Every which way and in all weathers. Well, you get what you pay for, don't you?

I flip my fly wings and soak up the July heat like I did beside the pool in Lanzor. The irony of being a fly. Filthy things. I spent my life after them with that plastic swat thing. They swarm around me now. *Find True North* they buzz into my non-existent ears.

Speaking of which. This wait for the Pearly Gates is a bit of a surprise. I thought I'd be shown the way by now instead of buzzing around like this. Where is the great Peter? It's been a few days. There must be some reason. Maybe the lift is full and there's a multitude waiting to get in. I'll bide my time.

'This heat is nice.' Fusspot is leaning into the back of the garden seat and putting her face to the sun. 'Mother defied cancer. She never acknowledged she had it.'

'She'll defy death too,' Loopy Loop replies, putting on sunglasses. 'She won't be getting into that grave anytime soon.'

I'm distracted by one of the flies beside me. It's carrying a child. I won't be having any truck with that. Nine months was enough to carry any of them. I hated it. Picked at my food to stop the relentless rise of swell. I never wanted children. I told them often enough.

'Do we mention she had no truck with political correctness?' That's what Fusspot is saying now.

They are on about my opinions. Like those babies buried in the Tuam cemetery. They took umbrage when I said those babies wouldn't mind where they were buried and what was the fuss anyway? When you're a nurse you've no room for that kind of sentimentality.

'Her tongue would slice you open. Rip into ya. Wasp tongue wickedness,' Loopy Loop says with a smirk. 'What do you think she'd make of that in her obituary?'

I reared them too soft. That was wrong. Listen to them now sitting on the garden seat taking in the sun. You'd think they'd have more to do. Anger wells up inside me. They jump up together as the back of my garden seat disintegrates behind their backs.

'Ancient thing,' Fusspot says, swatting me out of the way. 'Rotted through.'

Red Squirrel Days

Noelle Lynskey

On red-squirrel-days I am lighter in the world
or maybe the world is lighter on me,
no weight of missing out on blackberry time
or guilt of failed-to-set-gooseberry days.
Those jammy days, when my bushy tail
sets me up to take on a cloud-filled scape
full of my should-have-got-up-earlier dawns

On red-squirrel-days, alert and sharper,
balanced on any branch, head cocked to the sun
able to carry the heft of life's burdens,
I stash its secrets in the well of my drey,
store lines and rhymes in the tufts of my ears.
Miles away from sweet-briar times,
those I-wish-I'd-never-got-up kind of days

Though I try to face the trunk of such days,
embrace the girth at just the right angle,
set my gaze skyward, scale for the sky,
take a leap and trust my landing is sound,
skirt the forest's canopy at full stretch,
stash the freedom for far-too-often days
honed by hum-drum moments skittering by,

where being human, to be ourselves,
is to be erring,
                    sometimes forgiving,
hoarding the red-squirrel-days.

Untitled

Eamonn Lynskey

was only ever meant
to last a moment   reckoned

against the stars   or stones
      trees even   : this emergence

from a tunnel   speeding
towards another   rounding

hair-pin bends   never
seeing what's ahead

  careening wildly towards
an unknown destination

      well   : unknown to you
          and slowing now and then

  allowing people on
or off   till suddenly

it's you off   luggageless
  alone the rearlights fading

   maybe music playing
     seraphim descending

singing out your name
maybe   or maybe not

Ever Since You Left I Have Spent Every Moment With You

Shannan Mann

Do you stop strangers and ask them to walk with you? I do.
Where are you going? they ask. The less adventurous ones ask if
they need to carry sunscreen or snowsuits. When I was taught math,
I focused on subtraction. I leave out anything that could make them say
no. These strangers are not strangers to the people I have pulled them away
from. Soon, their old lives catch up to them. One of them, after a block,
tells me they really need to finish the grocery shopping. Another says,
I have a spouse and kids at home, and the dog shit needs to be scooped up
in composted-banana bags. The one with purple hair tells me about her coffee
enema and we stand in awkward silence that stretches like a cat. Another
makes guns out of his fingers, bolts away. A few, though, walk with me
for weeks. They don't even care to tie their shoelaces. I like them best.
They worry about ending the walk, and I offer grace. Tell them
endings are a conspiracy aired by God. That God is a myth created
by the first man. The first man is a lie told by the first woman.
The woman a rumour spread by the original amoeba. At this point
they are really nervous. They ask me the way back and I shrug.
I let them go. I walk alone. I allow everything to happen. I believe
in fate. I believe nothing is real unless you believe it is real.
I try to warn people, nourish dreadlocks, then lose all my hair.

The new year arrives and my resolution is nudity. I move states,
no longer solid, I live in liquidity, boiling to fugue. I think of you.
You are still my emergency contact. When you were around, I saw you
in stasis. Now that you are gone, I see you as rust on nails, ripples
in potholes, dust colonizing everything I once owned.

Birdswing

Deirdre Shanahan

FROM WHERE WE SIT AT THE TOP of the barn you get a hit of the smouldering heat across the sky and wheat fields and nobody knows we're there. The air is hazy but we can see for miles and know what is going on in the village; the time of deliveries to the farm, who's visiting the doctor or the number of cars parked at the restaurant where my mum works. And no one knows we come here, certainly not Helena's parents. Maybe Davin. We let our legs drip over the side of the bales where the wooden slats stop and leave a gap, but if one of us fell we'd be done for. Smashed in the head. Broken leg or arm. We sit back against the bales. Scratchy straw under our skin, the dry smell of the sun. The dope of heat hangs while I finger a tattered page of *Vogue* Helena sneaked from her house.

'Mum looks like her.' Helena points to a tall woman in a flowy dress against an ornate building of white stone with columns. Roman or something.

'Italy, maybe. She went the year before I was born. Showed me all these photos. She used to wear false eyelashes.'

Helena said her mum rode horses when she was a girl, but the few times I've seen her she was sleek and stylish.

'I'd love eyes like that.' The close-up has lashings of blue, going to turquoise and lavender, curving with a sprinkle of glitter at the corner of the lid. In the yard Davin slopes around when he should be seeing to the machinery, oiling tractors or something. That's what he's paid for. He leans against the wall of a shed and puffs on his cigarette, though no one's allowed to smoke in the yard. His hair is lanky thin. He mostly ignores us but I've seen his eyes. Deepest brown with flecks of rust like a fox. His corduroy jacket is thin at the elbow. His tartan shirt is thready. The hems of his jeans are ridged with mud. Jug sniffs the ground and Davin snaps his fingers, making Jug rise on his hind legs. Jug totters and Davin raises and lowers his hand like a conductor till the dog settles and when Davin walks off, he looks over his head to check if Jug follows.

When I'd asked Davin what he does after work, he batted me away with a slinky smile. He knows I live across the fields in a tight cottage at the corner of the lane with my mum, but he gives nothing away. He hasn't got a car. He only drives the van for the farm to deliver equipment and go to agricultural fairs. He could give me a lift home except I've never asked. But I'd like to sit in the front. Have his eyes turn on me in their sulky way. Get them to smile. His hands, though grimey, fluttering across the steering wheel.

Helena flicks through the back pages, examining bags, jewellery and shoes. She hasn't said when we can go to her room to try out make-up and I can't see why not as her parents aren't around. Davin slopes out of sight. His scratchy footsteps sound until he comes round the side towards the big shed where stocks of fertiliser are kept.

'You never know where he is. And he has a face like a dog.' Helena lays down the mag.

She can't either really think that, because once she said he was neat.

From the top of the barn, on the squiffs of scratchy straw, we see horses in the field opposite but they're not Helena's. The afternoon idles. From the shed, tractors groan and stall. Davin is testing attachments: weed cutters, forks to turn up the earth, the seeders or the chocks of steel forks to pull up crops.

Helena suggests we take out the tractor for a drive, so we slip down the ladder, kicking off strands of hay, and reach the corner of the field. She's been driving since she was 10. If we had worn jeans it would be easier but with shorts, dry mud scrapes my thigh. The tractor growls forward and Helena lets slip the wheel through her hands.

'Your dad teach you?'

'Him and whoever else was around,' she says.

The fields are edged with new fences, slats of light wood.

'Did he make those?'

'Who?' she asks.

'Davin.'

'He couldn't. He's not a carpenter.'

'Farmhand?'

'Something like that.'

Most lads have moved for work in town or gone to college. Davin lives with his dad. Only the two of them and he works long hours into the evening. She zig-zags across the field, while I hang on, leaning into the cab, its flap of a door going back and forth against my stomach. The engine chugs as if it needs seeing to. She takes a path across the field to the woods which aren't her dad's, and stops the engine in a ragged gruff of soil.

We descend near a barbed-wire fence. I hold down a section with a stick so Helena can step over and she does the same for me. In a clearing, tyres lie on their sides and bust cans are scattered.

Trees are scratchy dry and up high there's a fritter of birdsong. We breathe more easily and Helena sinks to the spread of dry leaves and tricks of tiny twigs. In the middle of a circle of trees, their gnarled roots like old ladies' fingers, lie the cinders of a fire, shuffly flakey black dead shards of wood. Water bottles are squeezed and bulge with heat. A smell of plastic smokes. I stir the remains with a stick, churning up bits and wonder who made the mess. Making fires is not allowed.

'This shouldn't be here.'

'None of it should.' Helena kicks into the leaves.

I poke and black dust rises. When I was a kid, I found Mum in the kitchen after Dad left, holding letters over the gas hob. I couldn't see her face but heard her cry. Later she told me they were cards and notes he'd sent, weights she wanted to do away with.

She lies back and the sun shimmers on her face. Flickers of shadows around her nose and ears. She tans easily and her legs are long. Davin walks towards the shed and I can see why Helena might think he's muddy and squalid. He's probably unhygienic.

'What does he do all day?'

'Lots of stuff. Anything Dad tells him. On a farm, there's always something. 'Specially,' Dad says, if you've livestock.'

Davin leans against the shed, lights a cigarette and slips the lighter in his back pocket. He inhales and catches me looking down. He gives a kick back to the wall and strides off.

Helena kicks off her sandals and lies against the straw, playing with her phone. Through gaps in the side of the barn I see her dad draw up in his new flashy jeep. His voice rises. And Davin's …

'You seen what my dad bought Mum.' She pulls out a pendant from under her T-shirt.

'A kind of diamond?'

'Amber. It's got insects. Buried in stuff from the trees.'

'Why'd you take it?'

'She wouldn't give me any more money.'

The stone is a bed of fire, with bits of insects which must've been alive. Helena stands and brushes herself down, hiding the pendant under her top. I'd never have jewellery. Nothing of value. Mum has only bracelets and necklaces of plastic beads from craft fairs. Small boxes of papiermâché for paste pearl ear-rings. I wonder if Dad gave her stuff. If he left her with anything other than me.

Mum returns to work the next week and I go to the farm on an evening before the light declines and the barn is coolly dark. Telegraph lines stretch for miles with swallows gathered for flight. Summer will end, kicking us out and back to school. I still haven't been to her room. I don't know what to put on my eyes. Helena lounges against the hay on a blanket. She's wearing the tight leopard-print trousers and has ear-pieces in, so I wave.

'Oh.' She pulls out the plugs. 'Your mum better?'

'Gone back to work, anyway.' The struts of the ladder are broken and splintered as I step up. 'What've you been doing?'

'Here mostly. In and out to town.' She shrugs her loose lavender T-shirt off the side of her shoulder. The other sleeve rides up and her tummy shows through the thin fabric. And the marks on her arm. An imprint of circles like stars. Grey smudges digging her skin. Cigarette burns. Who's done them, I'd like to know but daren't ask. Up here. Jug barks.

'That dog never shuts up.' She pulls a make-up bag from behind her. 'Wanna see this? Mum's stuff but she won't notice.' She props up a mirror on a bale of straw. 'This is what you have to do.' She purses her lips into an O like the soft mouth of a fish I'd won once at a fair. She smoothes on the lipstick, edging close to my lashes for a clean line.

'Yeah, makes you look different.'

'It's "Flare".' Her skin is paler, her eyes sharper and dark. 'Have a go.' She hands me the lipstick and holds up the mirror. I try to apply it as she has but I smudge above my lip. 'You'll get better with practice. And I've got this.' She shows me a slim pencil like a wand and pulls off the top to reveal a point like a felt tip. 'Eyeliner. Look in the mirror. I'll show you. Close your eyes.' She holds my shoulder to steady herself, and crouches in, her breath nippy with concentration. The tip slides across my lid. 'Now the other one.' She swaps shoulders. 'The trick is to make a flick at the end, like the wing of a bird, my mum says. See, you're flying.' She laughs, rolling back on her heels. The mirror shows me the way she said. There is a flick like a sweep.

'Thanks.'

'You can do anything with this.' She waves the pencil. Lines and brows. You can borrow it if you want and practise.'

'Thanks. I won't be around tomorrow, though. Have to help my mum.'

'Whenever. Mine's got loads and she says black is best for me.'

I speed off, even though I can't see when I'll need this. Not the places I go. I'd like to know how to use it.

Two days later, up at the farm, I slip into the yard.

'Helena,' I call but not loud in case it alerts her parents.

There's no one around. Not even the dog. And the yard is tidier. Bags of sand are stacked one end and the shed doors are shut. Jug is chained to his place. He barks. His teeth are hard white. The eyeliner wand sinks in my pocket. I used it but couldn't get the hang and made a lot of mess. Nothing in the way of the right shape. If I could keep it for long I might. If she let me.

Helena's not here. Or Davin. I clamber up to the loft of the barn, but it's empty. Maybe she's gone to town? Or had to go out with her mum? When I descend, the rungs are rickety thin and I skip the last two. The struts are worse than useless. Helena should tell her dad. No one else will. The yard is empty except for Jug who calmly lies on his front paws. There're voices. Davin. And another rising to a small laugh. Her. Someone says, 'no' with a giggle which subsides. A whimper. Low voices. And it falls low and quiet. Only traffic murmuring in the distance on the tide of summer already leaving.

Rain

Winifred McNulty

when   but
        but flat
        but
then
do dum
dun di   gulp
tam ton tat
plum fall splat
bit bot beat beak   peck peck
dum dum din dip deck
dot dum   bit it mit
dot pluck plum

from trees   rain drops fall like words
messages fat as plums on the tin roof of the shed   a first pluck
on a string   a voice splintering on the phone   a rhythm of dusk
beat pluck plum thrum bedum   sometimes
there are gaps   then   the evening swells with rain   trees meadows
darken   a single light like the moon in a neighbour's window
we will not escape ache   of body   or longing   damp sump fill
spill   entering skin   swelling under bone
shifts thoughts to squall   unable to resist damp leak drip mist
if only a small piece of this   would fall elsewhere
                  on the dry lands

Bottle Bairns

Pauline May

Let me tell yer 'ow I shared me crisps
with our Liam fer our breakfast –
walkin' 'im ter school –
'and-'oldin' fer the road.

Let me tell yer 'ow teacher said
I weren't listenin' –
an' were reet too – nee chance.
Me head were back round at ours.
'ow's our mam? What's she doin' now?
D' yer nah what I mean?

Let me tell yer 'ow I'm gerrin' big now.
Eight years old an' gerrin' big now.
Up at six – ter quiet like, quiet like,
garn round the cupboards for them bottles an' them cans.
And hoy what's left, that sweet an' sticky stuff,
down the sink – while she sleeps an'
snores an' sleeps like she always does now
on an' on.

Let me tell yer 'ow I were shocked at home time
that she's got there ter pick us up,
ter garn back ter ours.
But then we'd 'ad ter wait outside Mini Mart
An' could 'ear all the clinkin'
from 'er plastic bags from out the door.

Let me tell yer 'ow we garn back 'ome
an' then Mam sez there might be some biscuits
fer our tea. An' then I 'eard the door
an' Shirley – that new social worker –
come in – all eyes – looking 'ard at everything –
like camera eyes.
An' Shirley 'ad a reet big box –
emergency from food bank place, she said.

An' let me tell yer 'ow Liam an' me,
we joined 'ands – an' danced an' sang
an' sang an' danced
round that box now
on an' on.

Wanted

Paul McCarrick

Non-fussy male looking
for non-fussy female
willing to provide poetic
inspiration and possible amusement
on an hourly or daily basis.

Non-serious smoker desired,
with a welcoming attitude
to second- and third-hand fumes,
yet must be open to light up
walking down the Champs-Élysées
or 5th Avenue or Moore Street
while saying something like isn't this wonderful,
to be alive at this exact moment with you
or other vaguely romantic statements.

Must have a heart deep like Lough Derg,
morals as long-standing as the Shannon,
Lee, and Barrow, with a joie de vivre as
reliable and changeable as a calendar.

Looking for those of a loose
religious devotion or simply
to a day of rest, an affinity
with the continental style
of breakfast as well as an
unassuming aptitude for
European-style love-making.

And although the ability
to enjoy life is encouraged,
those who are ill or close to death
can also be desired. But if very far along,
deathbeds must be provided on a personal basis.

Both dog- and cat-people are welcome to apply.

There is an Old Woman

Alan McMonagle

Lives by herself at the top of a hill
in a house with a yellow door. 'I'm perished,'
she says each time she steps into the world.

Draws water from an ancient pump. A backyard boudoir
is where she powders her nose. When she looks
in her mirror it upsets her that no one is there.

Her neighbour is some crazy man's daughter.
The postman is a spy and has a method.
Her great ambition is to meet someone better than herself.

'Have I a nice speaking-voice?' she asks her Sweet Afton.
'I might join a singing-girl band,' she tells her idle TV.
'Ah, get down off your cross and use the wood,'

she calls out to the man on the Easter soap.
At mass she sucks Eskimo mints loudly,
tells the priest currant buns have souls.
At Bingo she sticks pins into a man she used to know.

Her summer hobby is taking mushrooms
from the judge's field. Along country roads she gurgles
Cidona, listens to the yarrow sigh.

Her favourite meal is six sandwiches
with something different in each of them.
Owning nothing takes up the rest of her time.

By the autumn stream she devours chocolate emeralds,
hides the wrappers inside a hollowed oak,
makes promises to visit them one day.

At night, in a basin of sudsy water, she washes
dishes, cups, her hands and teeth. The dishes are placed
on a frowning shelf. The teeth go in a glass jar.

In her bedroom she pees in a pot
and speaks with God. 'I am persecuted,'
she hisses at the children she never had.

Come Christmas Eve she takes a slow sherry
in McMorrow's pub. She waits for someone
to think of her. She forgives the mirror.

Housekeeping

Sarah Meehan

Last night
     the moon
was stacked on the washerwoman's rack
amongst the tilted dishes
        drying from dinner.

    Today
it rained and I realised she'd mended all the holes
in the canopy where water poured through
      the leaves,

and the blades of grass
stood straight as spires
where she'd brushed
the knots from the lawn – but

the lake was covered in pocks
like toothpaste splatter

   and the paths need mopping

and the wheat braiding

    and the webs patching

though she can't do any of this while she's up there
rubbing Silvo
        on the stars.

Catching the Ferry

Gerard Smyth

On the night before we sailed
we stopped in Wales
in a guesthouse good enough
for one-night-only.
The room was out-of-date.
The furniture and furnishings
were vintage 1910.
The nylon sheets crackled
when we lay down on them.
It was hard to breathe
in the dusty evening heat
trapped between the four walls
and the ceiling.
The all-night coming and going
and pushing at the door
was as sinister as that movie
made by Hitchcock in his heyday.
The sound of the dumb waiter
started early in the morning.
The breakfast plates held breakfasts
cooked the day before.

Our waitress had the shakes,
dropped ash onto the table
and told us it was raining,
that it always rained in Wales,
in the valleys, on the peaks.
So we took the wet roads out
to where the Irish Sea was waiting.

Notes on Naming

Audrey Molloy

My daughter tells me that the colour orange
is named for the fruit it resembles,
not the other way around.

The Droste effect, I tell her, is called after
not an artist or philosopher but a brand
of cocoa powder;

on the label, a woman in a wimple holds a box
of cocoa and the woman on its label
holds the same, mise en abyme,

and so it goes, this nested narrative. I tell her
that I follow on a line of eldest daughters
all named Hannah. If I squint my eyes,

I see their forms unfolding, hand-in-hand, diminishing
like paper dolls to the horizon and beyond.
My mother – a Hannah too –

broke the line and chose a name she loved for me.
Grace eats her orange, slice by slice. She asks
what does Hannah mean? I tell her

Hannah means favour. It means grace.

The Crannóg Questionnaire

Alison Wells

How would you introduce yourself as a writer to those who may not know you?

I write flash fiction, stories and novels on the literary, occasionally surreal, side and sometimes straying into speculative fiction. I studied social psychology so recurring themes in my writing are how social phenomena influence the individual, how belief can become contagious, how people can convince themselves of anything.

When did you start writing?

There were a couple of standout moments in my childhood (aged 8) and in adolescence when feedback from a teacher and a school short story prize sponsored by the *Kerryman* newspaper gave me so much pride and reinforced my desire to write. During my Leaving Cert year, I had to keep throwing a manuscript further and further under the bed to stop distraction. In 2000 my first son was born and from then on I combined writing in earnest and raising him and three more children. In 2009 I was nominated for a Hennessy Award for my short story *Bog Body* and writing has remained central in subsequent years.

Do you have a writing routine?

I wish I could give a definite yes ... I've written my Head Above Water blog since 2009 on finding time and headspace to write. Around that time a group of us founded the 5am writeclub online. Early mornings worked well alongside raising young kids. In 2015 my young family and I worked together to build a writing cabin in the garden. This proved a great place to find quiet and let ideas percolate. Now back at work full time I find it harder to write consistently. While I've been able to motivate myself to do daily dance routines, learning streaks in Irish on a language app and the Couch to 5K, gamifying the writing process into a routine is more difficult. I've completed the NaNoWriMo (50,000 words in a month) but I think it's important to find a balance between blind production for the sake of it and writing in a more sustainable and heartfelt way, so I am working on that.

When you write, do you picture somehow a potential audience or do you just write?

I try as much as possible to write from the inside out, to get into the character and place and see things through their eyes, imagine myself inside their physicality, like acting. Writing requires abandon and vulnerability, once you imagine an audience, you lose that.

Some writers describe themselves as planners, while others plunge right in to the writing. Would you consider yourself a planner or a plunger?

Definitely more a plunger, following the thread of an idea and internal momentum of the characters. This works pretty well for short stories, then you can edit, refine and cut. However where novels are concerned, unfettered plunging has led to a forest of material and no clear path. Now I start with an initial exuberance but have learned to stand back early in the process, write a possible synopsis and chapter plan and work the material into that.

How important are names to you in your books? Do you choose the names based on liking the way they sound or for the meaning? Do you have any name-choosing resources you recommend?

Yes, names are important, for sound and meaning and they can be constantly surprising or evocative – for example the surnames Memory or Bright. They need to be memorable, depict what a character is and stands for – without completely hammering the point home.

I focus more on character names in novels than short stories. Many of my short stories are told from a more close-up perspective inside the person's head so names may either not be used or be less loaded with significance. In my novels, I use names to evoke ideas and personality, for example the characters Anise Fish and Benedict Cleaver. Anise is a spice with a scent of aniseed or liquorice and Anise Fish is quirky and rooted in the natural world. Benedict Cleaver is a seemingly charming man with a more sinister, darker side.

A huge part of my childhood in Kerry was spent making up stories using objects or cut-out people from Bunty magazines as characters, but often my two sisters and I starred as our own heroines/heroes of the moment. My alias in some of these adventures for some reason was Walburga Radegund. I found these names in the 1954 *Naming Baby* book by Eugene Stones that our parents used. According to the book, Walburga means 'powerful protection' and Radegund 'counsellor of war' – so these must have been epic quests! This baby's name book is a simple resource I still use but looking at the credits of TV shows or browsing through genealogical sites can throw up unexpected treasures.

Is there a certain type of scene that's harder for you to write than others? Love? Action? Erotic?

I think it's more general than that. As long as the type of scene is relevant, earns its place and makes sense in terms of the story, I'm happy to give it a go. It's in any situation where I perhaps have more research yet to do about the location or the subject matter and it doesn't feel authentic, I start to feel like an imposter, self-doubt threatens to paralyse me. However, having said that, one member of my writing group writes thrillers with complex political machinations and all the technical elements that go along with being or avoiding an assassin. I wouldn't know where to begin!

Tell us a bit about your non-literary work experience, please.

In the past I've worked as a technical writer and HR manager. After taking time out to raise my four children I started work four years ago as a library assistant in public libraries in Dún Laoghaire-Rathdown County Council. First I worked in the Lexicon library, the largest public library in Ireland which also doubles as a cultural centre and theatre space, then I was transferred to the beautiful Shankill library – a cozy library that has a warm, community feel.

What is absolutely fantastic about working in the library is seeing what books and writing mean to readers. This was particularly poignant when we were sending out books to 'cocooners' from closed libraries and listening to their stories. The connection afforded by the service and the ability of a book to alleviate a very lonely and frightening time for many was something I feel very moved by and proud of still. Public libraries are a powerful and free force for good with connection, information, education and the absorption of a good book at their heart. The first story in my debut short story collection just out is inspired by that time at the library during Covid; the main characters connect and find some sort of solace out of the difficult events of their lives through books.

Of course, being surrounded by books all day is both a privilege and a temptation. On the creative side libraries are fantastic for those serendipitous finds tucked away that, for a writer, can inspire new work.

What do you like to read in your free time?
Mainly fiction but also books on psychology and neuroscience, particularly by Rick Hanson, as I am fascinated by how the mind works and how we can develop equanimity against the travails of life and creative resilience. At the moment, I find medical memoirs consoling, they look at the big questions in life, what gives life meaning, how medicine can perform miracles and whether it always should, authors like Henry Marsh and Rachel Clarke are always enlightening. Also, I highly recommend Susan Orlean's fascinating account of the history of the Los Angeles library.

What one book do you wish you had written?
I'm a great fan of the steady, beautiful work of Jon McGregor. *Reservoir 13* is a novel with an unusual point of view – that of the village – and its language is gorgeous. However *Dombey and Son* by Charles Dickens was the first novel that made me realise that a book could make you cry.

Do you see writing short stories as practice for writing novels?
No, I don't. I see different forms of writing nested in each other, for example I also write a lot of flash fiction where you use a handful of words to make an enduring impact, much like poetry. A short story has a fantastic, standalone, singular quality. I fell in love with reading novels so I've always been drawn to writing them. On one or two occasions, I've written a slightly longer story that then turns out to be the blueprint of a novel. For example my novel *The Exhibit of Held Breaths* (about how a strange exhibit affects the life of its reluctant curator and the residents of a 1980s town) which was a finalist in the Irish Centre's Novel Fair was fully encapsulated in the short story version I wrote originally. Each form has lessons to offer other forms, but one does not pre-empt another.

Do you think writers have a social role to play in society or is their role solely artistic?

Yes, writers have a social role. Writers can enlighten, inform and warn about injustice, censorship, dictatorship, war and other threats on personal, social and global levels. To strive to ensure that we interrogate our prejudices and assumptions we need opportunities to see life from other perspectives; writing books can provide those opportunities to readers. One stand-out book I read recently was *The Overstory* by Richard Powers – a book about trees and the climate crisis. This novel was able to make a very human and moving story through an array of characters – and through trees as characters – out of a pressing social and global issue.

Tell us something about your latest publication, please.

Random Acts of Optimism is my debut short story collection published by Wordsonthestreet in September 2023. It consists of 15 stories, ranging from poignant to laugh-out-loud, revolving around the protagonist's acts of optimism in the face of life. There are challenges from the humdrum to touching, to the more sinister and dramatic. We have the age-old story of the plumber who doesn't show up, zest for life in the face of a cancer diagnosis or prejudice, an elderly couple ridding an island of inconvenient dinosaurs, an astronaut who finds meaning in a cup of tea and family on his return home. The stories were written over a number of years from 2008 and this debut book signifies my own act of optimism in continuing to write and strive for publication over a long period of time!

Can writing be taught?

I think that a more coaching environment is preferable to a set of proscribed dos and don'ts, although a Jericho Writers workshop on self-editing gave me specific skills, particularly around point of view and psychological distance. So yes, there are technical issues that can be taught. Personally, I'm most interested in developing and encouraging creativity in general and confidence in a person's idea of themselves as a writer and persistence in their goals.

Have you given or attended creative writing workshops and if you have, share your experiences a bit, please.

I've attended workshops, for example as part of Mia Gallagher's Farmleigh residency where the participants focused on emerging novel work and also, as mentioned, a Jericho Writers workshop on self-editing. It's both challenging to put your work out there for critique but also very affirming to have your work and you as a writer taken seriously and I particularly like the workshop vs class for that. I've given classes to adults in the past but most recently offered creative writing workshops to children as part of my library job. There's so much you can learn from both attending and giving classes or workshops and it's often not what you expect – I've found my own enthusiasm for the creative process to be invigorated and my confidence in my own techniques and ability to be revived. I have a background in psychology and plan to give further classes on creative resilience and personal resourcefulness.

Finally, what question do you wish that someone would ask about your writing, and how would you answer it?
I think the question might be 'why should your writing continue to be published?' And I think the answer is tied up with the beauty of small presses who take a chance on unknown authors and good writing that might not always fit into standard shapes or trends. I have further writing, that I am proud of, stories and novels that – despite my own self-doubt – I do believe would connect with a reading audience and that I hope someone will take a chance on in the future.

Artist's Statement

Cover image: *Révérence, 2017,* by Julie D'Amour-Léger

Julie D'Amour-Léger was born in Caraquet, New Brunswick, in 1963. At the age of twelve, she began to explore photography. She continued her studies at the Université de Moncton and Concordia University in Montreal, where she obtained a BA in visual arts in 1986. She became a stills photographer, working in the film and television industry.

After living in Montreal for twenty-two years, she returned to Acadia in 2007. From her small house overlooking Caraquet Bay, she soaks up the air and light of her maritime surroundings. Landscapes, birds, and animals are her subjects of choice. Two exhibitions were created directly from her home, *From my Window* (2015) and *Crows: Black on White* (2017). Her photographic exhibition *Renardises* captured her bond with a group of wild foxes and was shown in Caraquet in 2016. Since 2019, she has been photographing the people involved with the fishing industry in the Acadian Peninsula, which will be the subject of her next exhibition and book.

In addition to her professional activities, D'Amour-Léger pursues various photographic projects connected to her immediate environment. With an intense focus on the local, she is moved by the authentic beauty of the landscape and the living creatures that surround her. Her poetic and carefully crafted images testify to her attachment to the nature and character of north-eastern New Brunswick – a sensibility that she always carries with her.

Biographical Details

Ivy Bannister has published collections of poetry and stories, and a memoir. Several of her radio plays have been broadcast. She has won the Francis MacManus and the Hennessy awards.

Lucy Bleeker is a Galway-based writer. Her one-act play *The Baggage* won the Best Writing Award at the Jerome Hynes One Acts Series 2023 as part of the University of Galway's Theatre Week. She was selected as one of the Irish Writing Centre's Young Writer Delegates at Cúirt 2023 and presented her short play *Bookshop* at the YWD showcase. She was listed for the Cúirt New Writing Prize for Poetry 2023. Her poetry has appeared in *New Word Order*.

Liam Carton writes fiction, poetry, and songs. His work has been published in *All World's Wayfarer* and *The Antihumanist*. instagram @liamcartonwrites

Louise G Cole writes poetry and short fiction and is a 2018 Hennessy Literary Award winner. In 2021. She was awarded a Literature Bursary by the Arts Council of Ireland.

Carolina Corcoran's work has appeared in a number of journals, including *Arc*, *The New Quarterly*, and *Magma*.

Polina Cosgrave is a bilingual poet and Arts Council award recipient based in Ireland. Her debut collection *My Name Is* was published by Dedalus Press (2020). Her work features in the Forward Prize Book of Poetry 2022 and in numerous journals and anthologies.

Maureen Curran's collection *Home* was published by Revival Press in 2018.

Annie Deppe is the author of three volumes of poetry, most recently *Night Collage* (Arlen House, 2021).

Theodore Deppe is the author of seven books of poems, most recently *Riverlight*, from Arlen House. His work has appeared in *Poetry Ireland Review*, *The Stinging Fly*, *Poetry*, *Kenyon Review*, and the Pushcart Prize anthology.

Mairéad Donnellan's poetry has been widely published. She has been shortlisted in national poetry competitions including Cúirt New Writing Prize and Doire Press Chapbook Competition. Her poetry has been broadcast on RTÉ Radio 1. She was winner of the Francis Ledwidge Poetry Award in 2013. In 2016 she won the Trócaire/Poetry Ireland poetry competition. In 2018 she was awarded the Tyrone Guthrie bursary by Cavan Arts Office. She was selected for Poetry Ireland introductions in 2019. In 2021 she was appointed Poet Laureate for Bailieborough as part of the Poetry Ireland, Poetry Town Initiative.

Michael Farry's latest poetry collection, *Troubles* (2020), is published by Revival Press, Limerick. Previous collections were *Asking for Directions* (Doghouse Books, 2012) and *The Age of Glass* (Revival, 2017). He has also written and published widely on the Sligo experience of the Irish war of independence and civil war.

Maggie Doyle is the author of *Mountain Notes – A Nature Diary* (Magysfarm.co.uk 2021). She was shortlisted for the Seamus Heaney Award for New Writing in 2023 and has poems published in *The Blackbird Anthology* and the Poetry in Motion Community Anthology. She presents and produces *The Mountain Gate* podcast.

Susan Elsley's short fiction has been published in *The Storms*, *Fictive Dream*, *Northern Gravy*, *Postbox*, *PENning*, *Pushing Out the Boat* and *Northwords Now*. She was shortlisted for Moniack Mhor's Emerging Writer Award in 2019 and the Alpine Fellowship Writing Prize in 2023. susanelsley.com

Angela Graham's poetry collection *Sanctuary: There Must Be Somewhere* was published by Seren Books in 2022. Her poetry has been published in journals such as *The North*, *Poetry Wales* and *The Interpreter's House* and in anthologies including Dedalus Press's *Romance Options* and *Local Wonders* and Arlen House's *Washing Windows Too* and *Washing Windows III*. She won first prize for poetry in the inaugural Linen Hall Ulster-Scots Writing Competition in 2021. She has a poem in Poetry as Commemoration's Juke Box curation, May – July 2023. Her short story collection *A City Burning* (Seren Books, 2020) was longlisted for the Edge Hill Prize. @AngelaGraham8

Jessica Grene's work has been published in *Mslexia* and *Crannóg*. She worked in international humanitarian emergencies for a decade, before moving into the research sector.

Nicki Griffin's debut collection of poetry, *Unbelonging*, was published by Salmon Poetry in 2013 and was shortlisted for the Shine/Strong Award 2014 for best debut collection. *Crossing Places*, her second collection of poetry, was published by Salmon Poetry in 2017. A third collection is forthcoming.

Daniel Hinds won the Poetry Society's Timothy Corsellis Young Critics Prize. His poetry was commended in the National Centre for Writing's UEA New Forms Award, and has been published in *The London Magazine*, *The New European*, *Southword*, *Abridged*, *Poetry Bus Magazine*, *Ropes*, *Stand*, *Poetry Salzburg Review*, *Blackbox Manifold*, *The Honest Ulsterman*, and elsewhere. His poetry has also been broadcast on BBC platforms and the *Eat the Storms* podcast. Twitter: @DanielGHinds

Jennifer Horgan's work appears in various journals such as *Howl*, *Washing Windows III* and *The Honest Ulsterman*. Her debut collection is due in 2025 with Doire Press.

Karan Kapoor has been awarded or placed for James Hearst Poetry Prize, Frontier Global Poetry Prize, Rattle Annual Prize, Ledbury Poetry Prize, Julia Darling Memorial Prize, Red Wheelbarrow Prize, John & Eileen Allman Prize for Poetry,

Orison Anthology Award, and Literary Taxidermy Competition. The manuscript *Portrait of the Alcoholic as a Father* was a semi-finalist for the Charles B. Wheeler Poetry Prize. Poems have appeared or are forthcoming in *AGNI, North American Review, Poetry Online, Colorado Review, The Offing, Strange Horizons, Arts & Letters*, and elsewhere. karankapoor.co.in.

Carella Keil is a Canadian writer and digital artist. Her work has appeared recently in *Columbia Journal*, on the cover of *Glassworks* Issue 26, in *Superlative Literary Journal* (Mini-Saga Runner Up 2022), *Stripes Literary Magazine, Chestnut Review* and *Door is a Jar*.

Hugo Kelly has won many awards for his short fiction including the Cúirt New Writing Award and the Maria Edgeworth Short Story Competition. He has twice been shortlisted for the New Irish Writing Awards for Emerging Fiction and the RTÉ Francis MacManus Awards. His short stories have appeared previously in *Crannóg* and *The Stinging Fly* and have been broadcast on BBC Radio 4 and RTÉ Radio 1.

Aisling Keogh's short stories have been published in the *Irish Independent, The Honest Ulsterman, Wordlegs, Ropes, Bangor Literary Journal, A New Ulster, Crannóg* and in several anthologies. She was shortlisted for the Hennessy Irish Literary Awards in 2011, and also for the Doolin Writers Weekend Short Story Competition. She is currently working on her second novel.

Noel King's poetry collections are *Prophesying the Past* (Salmon, 2010), *The Stern Wave* (Salmon, 2013) and *Sons* (Salmon, 2015) and *Alternative Beginnings, Early Poems* (Kite Modern Poetry Series, 2022). He has edited more than fifty books of work by others (Doghouse Books, 2003 – 2013) and was poetry editor of *Revival Literary Journal* (Limerick Writers' Centre) in 2012/13. A short story collection, *The Key Signature & Other Stories*, was published by Liberties Press in 2017. www.noelking.ie

Anya Kirshbaum's work has appeared in *The Comstock Review* and *Cirque*, and was a finalist for the New Millennium Writing Awards.

Susan Lindsay has published three collections of poetry with Doire Press. Her writing has been published in journals and anthologies in Ireland and abroad. She facilitates conversations mediated by poetry and writes occasional blog posts at susanlindsayauthor.blogspot.com.

Noelle Lynskey completed her MA (Creative Writing) in UL in 2022. She was selected as Strokestown's Poet Laureate in 2021. She facilitates Portumna Pen Pushers and is artistic adviser to Shorelines Arts Festival.

Eamonn Lynskey is a poet and essayist whose work has previously appeared in leading magazines and journals including *Crannóg, Poetry Ireland Review, Southword, Cyphers*, and *The Irish Times*. His fourth collection, *Material Support*, was published by Salmon Poetry in 2023. www.eamonnlynskey.com.

Shannan Mann has been awarded or placed for the Palette Love and Eros Prize, Foster Poetry Prize, Peatsmoke Summer Contest, Rattle Poetry Prize, Pacific Spirit Poetry Prize and Frontier Award for New Poets. Her poems have appeared or are forthcoming in *The Literary Review of Canada*, *Poet Lore*, *Gulf Coast*, *Strange Horizons*, and elsewhere. https://linktr.ee/shannanmania

Mari Maxwell's work features in *Washing Windows III* (Arlen House 2023), and *Washing Windows Too* (2022). Her work is published in the *Poetry Jukebox STARS Curation*, part of the 2021 Belfast International Arts Festival. She received a 2020/21 Professional Development Award with the Arts Council of Ireland and a 2019/20 Words Ireland/Mayo County Council Mentorship.

Pauline May's work has appeared in many magazines including *Acumen*, *The Blue Nib*, *The Ogham Stone*, *The Writers' Cafe* and *Riggwelter* and in several anthologies.

Paul McCarrick's poetry has been published in *The Ogham Stone*, *The Stinging Fly*, *Poetry Ireland Review*, and most recently in the Poetry Ireland anthology *Vital Signs*. He was selected to take part in the 2019 Poetry Ireland Introductions Series. He is currently completing his first collection.

Alan McMonagle has written for radio and published two collections of short stories (*Psychotic Episodes* and *Liar Liar*). *Ithaca*, his first novel, was published by Picador in 2017, and was longlisted for the Desmond Elliott Award for first novels, the Dublin Literary Award, and shortlisted for an Irish Book Award. His second novel, *Laura Cassidy's Walk Of Fame*, appeared in 2020.

Winifred McNulty's poems have been published in *Poetry Ireland Review*, *Mslexia*, *Cyphers*, *The North* and other magazines. She has won the iYeats and Westport poetry prize and in 2022 was placed in The Red Line Poetry Competition. She has read her work on RTÉ and has received an Arts Council award to work on a poetry pamphlet.

Sarah Meehan's work has appeared in *Crannóg* and *Cordite Poetry Review* (Australia).

Audrey Molloy's debut collection, *The Important Things* (Gallery Books, 2021), was shortlisted for the Seamus Heaney First Collection Poetry Prize. *The Blue Cocktail* will be published by the Gallery Press in late 2023. She has a masters degree in Creative Writing from Manchester Metropolitan University. Her work has appeared in *The Stinging Fly*, *The Moth*, and *Poetry Ireland Review*.

Mike O'Halloran has published fiction in *The Sunday Tribune* and *Crannóg*. He is a member of Galway Writers' Workshop and is currently working on a novel.

Ilse Pedler won the 2015 Mslexia Pamphlet Competition. Her pamphlet, *The Dogs That Chase Bicycle Wheels* was published by Seren in March 2016. She was longlisted in the National Poetry Competition in 2018 and is the poet in residence at Sidmouth

Folk Festival. Her first collection *Auscultation* was published by Seren in 2021. www.ilsepedler.com.

Elizabeth Power has won or been placed in several international and national competitions and her fiction has appeared in numerous publications including *The Moth*, *Crannóg*, *Skylight 47*, *Trasna*, and *Force Ten*. Her poetry is published in the UK, US and Italy.

Deirdre Shanahan's collection of stories was published by Splice. She has been included in *The Best of British Short Stories* published by Salt. She was longlisted for the BBC Short Story Award in 2018 and in 2022. She has received an award from Arts Council England, and from The Society of Authors to undertake research in Africa. Most recently, she was longlisted for the Commonwealth Story Award and shortlisted for the Berlin Writing Prize. Toby Litt has selected one of her stories for inclusion in MIROnline.

Gerard Smyth is a poet, critic and journalist who has published ten collections of poetry, the most recent of these are: *The Sundays of Eternity* (Dedalus Press, 2020); *A Song of Elsewhere* (Dedalus Press 2015), *The Fullness of Time: New and Selected Poems* (Dedalus Press, 2010) and *The Yellow River* (with artwork by Seán McSweeney and published by Solstice Arts Centre, 2017). He was the 2012 recipient of the O'Shaughnessy Poetry Award from the University of St Thomas in Minnesota. www.gerardsmyth.com

Breda Spaight's poetry is widely published. Her debut collection, *Watching for the Hawk*, is published by Arlen House.

Mary Turley-McGrath is the author of four poetry collections: *New Grass under Snow* (Summer Palace Press, 2003), *Forget the Lake* (2014), *Other Routes* (2016), and *After Image* (2020) all from Arlen House. Her poems have appeared in recent anthologies, including: *Hidden Donegal* (2022), *Future Perfect* (2019), *The Strokestown Anthology* (2018), *Reading the Future* (2018), and *The Forward Anthology* (2011). She has won The Francis Ledwidge Poetry Competition and the Trócaire/Poetry Ireland Competition. She holds an M. Phil in Creative Writing from Trinity College Dublin.

Maureen Weldon is published in magazines, journals, anthologies, online and paper, including, *Crannóg*, *Poetry Scotland*, *Vsesvit Ukraine*, *Atrium*, *Ink Sweat & Tears*, *Dreich*, *Blithe Spirit*, *Journal of The British Haiku Society*. She has been featured by The Poetry Kit Caught in The Net. She has published eight books/pamphlets, her latest pamphlet *The Waking Hour* (2021) published by Red Squirrel Press.

Stay in touch with
Crannóg
@
www.crannogmagazine.com

Milton Keynes UK
Ingram Content Group UK Ltd.
UKHW030025040923
428004UK00012B/82